"2014"

Mom,
Merry Christmas
Love ya,
Charise

Village Fete

A novel by
Michele Deppe

Copyright © 2014 by Michele Deppe
ISBN-10: 1500997471
ISBN-13: 978-1500997472
This is a work of fiction. Names, characters, corporations, institutions, organizations, events, or locales in this novel are either the product of the author's imagination or, if real, used fictitiously. The resemblance of any character to actual persons (living or dead) is entirely coincidental. No part of this book may be reproduced, uploaded to the Internet, or copied without author permission.

For Tod with love, and for Barry M. Jones,
an author, curator, and creator of woodcraft

Chapter One

THE OLD WHITE van squeaked as it mounted the narrow stone bridge, its headlamps bouncing beams across the road as it came down the opposite side. Grumbling over cobbled streets, the vehicle rolled past the *Twinns*, an ancient pair of Tudor cottages on King Street. The cottages huddled behind a granite wall, which bore the name of the village, Burleigh Cross, in antiquated script. An otherwise insignificant village, Burleigh Cross kept a toehold in England's history simply for standing there, for time immemorial, amongst forgotten fields.

Burleigh Cross, Simon Whiston liked to say, had seen him born and bred and soonest fled. But here he was returning home like a waster.

Dusk was rapidly giving way to night, and it was too late for anyone to be about as he skirted the green, his van rumbling loudly in the late summer evening against the tall, dense trees. Standing at odds were the crumbling old church and the George & Dragon pub, which had always closed early on Mondays, and apparently still did. A weak light glowed in the post office. An end-of-season sale board was propped in the window of Goodchild's shop. Then came the half-empty row, a handful of shops and offices in the old mews.

Unexpectedly, Simon warmed with affection as he drove by the familiar shopfronts, but he smirked at the abandoned estate agents. The village's stone cottages, expansive Victorian houses, and farms all sheltered, more or less, the same families as they'd always done. London commuters bound for Victoria or Waterloo East station were efficiently based in Maidstone, a dozen country miles distant.

In a blink, he'd driven through the village. Grinning, he shook his head. Growing up his whole world had been encompassed here, barely a wide spot in a road used for going somewhere else.

Leaving the village proper the road lengthened up a hill, towards a thick border of beech crowned by the expansive night sky. As Simon's headlights swept around the first bend, his memory filled in Stanley Pugh's apple orchard, hidden in shadows beyond the hedge.

Instantly, the familiar scene changed.

Simon stood on the brakes. The tyres screamed into the darkness, the van's bumper scarcely missing a white, wolf-like creature that darted into the road. The silvery beast crossed the lane and disappeared into a break in the opposite hedgerow.

Then, something even more fantastic.

A woman appeared, running in the creature's wake. The van's headlamps shimmered against her scarlet gown, her long blonde hair was glazed by moonlight.

In a suspended moment, both the wolf-like creature and the woman were gone.

"What the…" Simon sat motionless, his mind replaying the scene. Baffled, he shifted the van and drove on.

Simon's vehicle crept between the winding, grassy verges. As the road levelled, his eyes swept back and forth, lest a wild animal pursued by an equally wild woman should again materialize in his path. A curve to the right, a soft left, and then the old farmhouse swung into view. He turned onto the gravel drive, followed its arc away from the house, and parked the van beside his father's old workshop.

The lantern by the farmhouse door spilled out a weak golden pool of light, but the house stood quiet. Simon eased slowly out of the driver's seat, his torso retaining the shape of a prawn. As his feet touched stone, he steadied himself by gripping the steering wheel. Best to come back later for his kit. His body clenched in pain, but he sucked in a deep breath and forced his shoulders to straighten. The drive from London had been a bit much. Nonetheless, no stooping allowed.

He shuffled, his hips sending hot shards of complaint up and down his sides. Simon stopped for a moment. Twenty-nine, but feeling nigh on 90, he'd learned the value of moving slowly on bad days. Having to go at a pensioner's pace flooded him with a sense of defeat, but his body quieted, the pain stabbed a little less sharply, and he imagined he was walking quite normally as he came to the front of the house. Trudging onto the low porch, he drew his childhood key from his pocket, turned the lock, and stepped through the old oak door.

The house wasn't slumbering as he'd thought. His sister sat at the heavy, scrubbed wooden table that had belonged to their grandmother. He could tell by the look on her face she'd witnessed his plodding procession through the room's far window, which framed a view of the workshop.

"Lorna."

"I thought you said the new medication was helping. You look fairly crippled to me."

"Lovely to see you, too, Sis."

Avoiding the firm chairs with woven-rush seats that stood around the table, Simon aimed for the soft, archaic, dark-gold velvet sofa in the sitting room that was as welcoming as a fat granny's lap. The late summer warmth had burned away hours ago, leaving the room chilly. Tiny arrows of pain shot upwards through his back and neck as he sank down onto the sagging cushions.

"I am sorry, Simon. It's really awful to see you like this. I thought those new tablets would do you a treat. You said you'd be all right, didn't you? But obviously not."

He'd expected as much. Simon hadn't seen his sister for two years or more, before everything in his life went reeling. He'd hoped to have this scene with her in the morning, when he felt less depleted from dealing with his creaking body all day.

Lorna Whiston pulled a face, brows weaving together. Her expression was familiar, and Simon braced himself. Her disappointment was easier to endure than the onslaught of empathy that was about to ensue. "I didn't expect you to look so poorly, Simon. That's cruel to say, I suppose, but you are quite changed, you know."

The cold room caused Simon to shudder. The truth was, he shared his sister's bewilderment. He'd studied his face in the mirror not a few times lately, feeling oddly remote as he noticed the gaunt curve beneath his cheekbones. There was no hint of the old fire he used to possess, and he had the odd feeling of not recognising himself. Perhaps worse was trying to fill his days without work.

His misfortunes came in rapid succession. First, the lawsuit came against him, crushing his business as well as his spirit, followed by the mysterious pain. His mind cast back to the night, two years ago, when illness abruptly took him hostage. He had gone to bed early, he and his wife both supposing that Simon was suffering from flu.

That night, in the space of a few hours, the pain throughout his body went from achy to agony. Clearly not the flu, he remembered telling his wife. Dominique's fear had been palpable. He remembered the wail of the ambulance, and how it took him a while to work out that it was coming for him.

Dominique hadn't come to the hospital during the days that followed. She wasn't with him when a specialist gave him the diagnosis. Simon's hip was full of fluid, he was told, which was pressing on his sciatic nerve, thus the pain; the long-term impact the arthritis would have on his life was uncertain. He was advised to rest, eat properly, and, above all, avoid stress. When he'd come home after four days in hospital, his wife wasn't there. So much for avoiding stress, he'd thought as he wandered the rooms of their large house, his footsteps echoing on the cold tile floors of the starkly decorated, modern rooms. That's when the truth came to him quite suddenly. His wife didn't love him any longer—and she hadn't for quite some time. Dominique hadn't encouraged him to spend more time at home. Why was that? He knew she was terribly independent, but he wondered how she'd filled her evenings. He couldn't remember her ever getting around to answering those sorts of questions when he'd asked them.

The divorce papers arrived with the legal bills; his business, his health, and his marriage all failed in the same breath.

He'd held out for as long as he could, and then phoned his sister. Simon told Lorna that he needed a place to stay. His money had run out, and he had to leave his flat. Here he was back in the village he'd sworn he'd never return to, trying to explain the whole bloody mess to a sister with whom he'd never gotten along.

"The medication was helping a bit, over the last year and a half. But recently the meds became worthless. I saw the doctor about a fortnight ago. As it happens, he had a new medication. So I gave it a go."

Simon looked away from his sister as he explained his latest calamity, resenting the kick that came when he was already down. "The thing I haven't told anyone else—is that I'd heard from a friend that Dominique had been having an affair when we were married. Honestly, I could hardly blame her. I was so seldom home. She had always been telling me how critical it was to keep the large orders coming in, how the first five years of laying a foundation for a business often determines one's success. I knew she wanted, more than anything, for me to be successful. She never talked about wanting anything for us—never mentioned kids, she never wanted to plan holidays; always steering me towards making the business work. Not to mention, she was spending money like water. I didn't really believe it before, that stress can make a person ill, however the doctor seemed to imply that had a lot of bearing on my condition."

Lorna's eyes welled with tears.

"I am sorry."

"No, don't apologise, Simon," his sister said. "I want to hear it all. Go on."

"Well. Two weeks ago, I was desperate for some relief. I'd only taken one dose of the new medication—from a sample packet given to me at the doctor's surgery. A few minutes later, I collapsed in front of my flat. I couldn't breathe. Someone passing by found me and rang for help, and I was taken to hospital. They said it was a reaction to the drugs. It wasn't too difficult to figure out my priorities, breathing being rather important, so I quit the medication, as well as the other tablets that weren't helping."

Lorna stared at him. His sister was rarely speechless, but she was coming to understand he'd been severely ill, more so than he'd let on during the several phone calls that had passed between them in as many years.

Simon cast about for something encouraging, but came up empty. Losing his wife, his business, and his health had been hell. He didn't particularly want to talk about the last 24 months, but he owed her an explanation. They had never been close. In fact, he'd found Lorna singularly irritating when he'd still been living at home. She returned his antipathy, yet she'd put aside their differences and offered their family's home to him. "I appreciate you letting me come home, Lorna."

His younger sister absently studied the table beneath her elbows, tracing a circular stain in the wood. "Only because you had nowhere else to go. Like an old dog." She turned to look down the room at him and grinned.

"I am glad you're not angry with me for—well, for cocking up my life, and turning up like this."

"Not yet." She rose from the table and stretched. "But give it a day or maybe less, and you'll probably have to set up house in the workshop."

"What a loving sibling you are."

"Naturally, dear Simon." She went to the tap and filled the kettle.

"Had quite a strange thing happen coming on this side of the village," Simon said, resorting to casual chat and stifling a yawn. "There was a white, wolfish looking animal, and a woman running after it. Utterly bizarre, I can tell you. They passed right in front of me and it was lucky that I was quick with the brake."

Lorna lobbed sugar into both teacups. "That's our resident witch."

"You can't be serious."

The kettle whistled and he watched as Lorna made their tea. He ought to walk over to claim his tea and join her at the table. But he just couldn't muster the courage to set his body ablaze again.

His sister seemed to sense this and brought their tea to the small sitting room. Simon was grateful for the kindness. She set his tea on a table in front of the sofa, then sat and tucked her feet beneath her, settling in like a contented cat on a navy blue and white winged chair opposite him. It was a chair he'd made, one of the first he'd upholstered; very ambitious given that it was a striped fabric and thus more difficult to match up at the seams. It had been a present for their mum on Mothering Sunday. Even now, he felt rather proud of having made it.

"Well I am serious, and it would seem you're hardly in a position to argue with me, now you've seen her haunting the lane." Lorna sipped her tea. "She came to Burleigh Cross two, maybe three, months back. Hung out a shingle at the old surgery, what used to be Dr. Clewely's before he moved closer to Maidstone. Calls herself a healer and uses herbs or something."

"And she's the resident sorceress, hmm? Potions and the like?" Simon took a deep quaff of tea. Mercifully, his sister had given him a mug, which was easier for his stiff fingers to embrace. His hand and wrist throbbed from holding the heavy ironstone, but the steam enveloping his face and sweet warmth on his tongue was worth the bee sting in his joints. The old sofa held him lovingly, and he grew more relaxed.

"Not only that. There were some odd rumours floating about. Hardly anyone's been to her lair to report what goes on there. The white dog's rather real though, I've heard it barking. It seems to escape a lot. She's forever running after it and bringing it home."

"Home?"

Lorna cradled her delicate china cup in both hands. "She's our neighbour. The Grahams' cottage was to let when she came. They're so often in the City now, what with the company he works for expanding offices in every possible direction." Simon reflected on the Grahams, whose cottage stood across the road. He was at school with David, who'd gone off to university and become an architect. David had made lots of upgrades to the cottage after his parents left to move closer to David and his wife in London. The Grahams hired Simon on to restore the charming old staircase, whose steps had worn away like broken teeth. Stair climbing had been effortless for Simon in those days.

"Finley and Peony are excited you've come. They'll be all over you in the morning, you know." It was touching to hear Lorna regard him with affection, particularly with regards to sharing her children's enthusiasm for their uncle. He'd always enjoyed an easy relationship with Lorna's kids on the few occasions they'd met. Simon would swoop down to the floor to play with them, while his French wife had stood by, distracted, silent, and evidently eager to return to London.

"I am looking forward to seeing how much they've grown." Simon's eyes began to water with fatigue.

"I went to Vandersteen's shop and traded some things for a storabed." Lorna gestured towards the tiny spare room at the back of the sitting room, the top of its doorway sliced across one corner where the stairs sloped up to the ceiling. "I know it's little more than a box room, but, mind you, you knew how it was going to be. I can't very well chuck the kids out of their rooms, or give up mine, you know." Her voice sharpened with a defensive edge.

"No, no, of course not, Lorna. I am glad of a roof over my head till I can get sorted. Cheers."

He remembered what Lorna had said, almost two years ago, when Dominique had gone. She'd thought her brother was a fool, letting his big house in London go to his wife in the divorce, not asking her for so much as a pound or an apology. Somehow, he still didn't regret that, even though without Lorna's hospitality he'd be homeless.

Lorna sighed, and rose to her feet. "'Night, Simon."

"Sweet dreams, my girl."

Chapter Two

THE NEXT MORNING Simon woke in his father's old study. Miracles never ceased, as he'd managed not to punch, kick, or otherwise maim himself on the sturdy desk or the wall, both of which loomed less than half a foot from the flanks of his short-stay bed. Likewise, it was a mercy that the bed had neither a footboard nor headboard, so that Simon's tall frame could stretch slightly over each end. He lay quietly for a few minutes, listening to his sister and her children speak to each other, and although their words were unintelligible, their muffled conversation gave comfort, as he was a man who hadn't enjoyed living on his own. The low hum of a TV could be heard, tuned to some children's program. Simon slowly pushed his right arm up along the wall, lifting the window blinds away from the glass with his hand. The sky was a deep blue with a few daubs of dazzlingly white, dense clouds like heaps of birthday cake frosting. The sun was most certainly blazing into the farmhouse kitchen, for there was a cool shadow over the back of the house, shielding Simon from the blinding light that would finger its way through the slats of the shade later in the morning. His arm grew heavy and he let it drop lightly onto his chest. Mornings were the most challenging part of the day. He dreaded the pain that would course through his body when he pushed his way out of bed. At least today there were other people for which he could carry on, instead of only being accountable to himself.

Slowly he sat up and then drew his knees up to his body, curving out the muscles in his back. He rubbed his eyes. His stomach grumbled; he hadn't had anything much to eat yesterday. His sudden hunger and the desire to greet the kids gave him an unaccustomed twinge of excitement. He fished on the floor for the jeans and shirt he'd worn yesterday. Dressing as though he were a passenger on a sleeper train, he drew on clothing while seated within the berth of the narrow bed, so as to avoid banging elbows and knees in the close confines.

Simon's nephew and niece were as sweet as lambs, greeting him with great hugs and lots of noise. They wanted to ask their uncle lots of questions, about London, and animals, and was he ever in the army, and they laughed at his jokes. Finally, Lorna sent Finley out to the van for Simon's bag, and Simon started up the stairs for a hot shower.

The sun had crept over the spine of the steeply pitched, tiled roof when Simon reappeared downstairs. Finley had joined his mates for the quarter-mile walk to the village to buy sweets from Goodchild's shop, one of the last summer excursions before the school term would resume, while Simon and Peony lingered over a hearty breakfast. Lorna had served loads of eggs, sausages, toast, and sweet, juicy slices of late August tomatoes from the rambling plant beneath the kitchen window. Simon ate more than he'd done in a long while.

Three year-old Peony sat on her uncle Simon's knee. She wiggled the muzzle of a plush giraffe close to his ear, making Gemma Giraffe to do the talking, as Gemma Giraffe wasn't nearly as shy. "Mummy called you a sponge. Do you've got gooseberry in you?" Peony's giraffe asked, while she plunged her pointer finger into his tummy.

"Oops, sorry," Lorna mumbled, as she wiped down the cooker.

Simon laughed and told Peony he was full of toast this morning and so was she. Peony giggled and she snuggled close.

"Bit of good news that I forgot to tell you last night," Simon said to his sister. "I've got a job interview. It'd be for teaching a course in wood working at the community college."

Lorna turned, drawing off her kitchen gloves. "Really? Simon, that'd be wonderful. I don't expect they pay much, but it'd be something along the lines of what you did before. Sort of."

Simon dropped his chin into Peony's soft curls and let out a sigh. She giggled, and then Gemma Giraffe said, "Moo." He thought about correcting her but wasn't quite certain what sort of noise comes from a giraffe. Simon blew a raspberry into Peony's hair, sending her into another fit of laughter.

He thought about what he might do with his day. Two years ago, there'd scarcely been enough hours in the day to keep up with the orders coming in for hand-crafted furniture. He'd had two-dozen people on the payroll. Putting in overtime was common practice.

"Down you get, Peony." Simon tried not to wince as his niece slid over his tender knee, wriggling her feet towards the floor.

"We're going to the shops," Lorna said, pushing Peony's hands through the sleeves of a light pink, gauzy jumper. "Do you need anything from the village?"

"No, thanks." He planted a hand on the table to hoist himself to his feet, grabbing his fizzy drink with the other. His fingers clenched and dented the plastic bottle as hot pain volleyed through his body. Lorna watched, stone-faced, as he manoeuvered towards the door. Simon could imagine what she might be thinking. Both of her children's fathers had left her as soon as they knew she was expecting a child. *She must feel cursed*, Simon thought, as now she had an unemployed, crippled brother under foot. He wanted to offer to do something around the house, but he couldn't trust his voice at the moment, so he walked out the front door ahead of she and Peony.

Walking out of the house, the balmy, late summer air revived his spirits. He made his way over to his father's old, timber workshop. Oakley Whiston had been a fair mechanic in his day, sorting out farm vehicles, cars, vans, motorcycles—anything with an engine, really. Mona had been a lunch lady; quiet, nurturing, and always close to Simon and Lorna during their years at the village school.

The workshop door was heavy. Hooking his palm around the metal handle, Simon leveraged his weight to roll back the large panel door. The greasy, dirty smell of the workshop brought it all back; the crunch of tyres coming and going on the gravel drive, the hiss of an air compressor, a jingle blaring from an old radio, the roar of engines coming to life as a result of his father's skill. It was hard to pinpoint exactly when things became unbearable, but Simon left home shortly after his sixteenth birthday. He'd wanted no more of his father's drunken outbursts, or anything to do with working in his father's garage.

He'd drifted from place to place, helping out at workshops—vastly different to his father's garage, for these were full of wood that manifested into furniture, fireplace mantels, crown molding and countless other forms—and he'd learned his trade as a carpenter. Simon loved the spicy, earthy smell of freshly hewn timber, the feel of solid tools in his strong hands, the proud sense of accomplishment that came with mending a loved old chair, or fashioning a wedding present that was destined to become a family heirloom. His body was powerful then, muscles hard from constant use and manual labor. His mind was quick with figures, and he got on well with a variety of people.

Now a teaching job seemed to be the only option. He wished he had some small piece of his work, such as a trinket box, or perhaps an ornate music stand, to show his prospective employer, but he didn't remember sending anything home to Lorna. And he'd brought nothing from London except clothes, some tools, and a wooden trunk—a gift from a fellow woodcrafter—full of personal items. Everything else had been sold to pay the lawsuit brought against him, and he'd simply let go a number of items to his employees and friends.

His father's workshop smelled of oil and was furred with spider's webs. There were two old cars, various rusted parts, and empty whiskey bottles. In the end, his father must've been beyond caring, to leave his empty bottles accumulating in the garage for anyone to see.

Simon had gone from home the year that his father became ill, and his sudden departure seemed to set in motion an eruption within the family. He'd later heard from his mates that Lorna had run away with a boyfriend shortly after their father's funeral. Some three or four months later, she'd discovered she was pregnant with Finley and returned to Burleigh Cross. When Lorna arrived at the farmhouse she learned, from a letter left on the kitchen table, that their widowed mother had moved to Australia to live with her only sister. Also gone were the family photographs, presents given to Mona from Oakley, and other mementoes of Mona's years in the farmhouse with her husband and two children. Having nowhere else to go, Lorna got a job, had the decorators in to transform her parents' bedroom, and prepared to have a baby on her own.

His father's old workbench was solid. It lured Simon, and immediately he began collecting rubbish from its surface and binning it. The pain in his hands screamed, but he didn't care. He needed to do something. Perhaps he would never be able to craft furniture again, but while he worked, he imagined his tools arranged in tidy boxes on the solid surface of the workbench, and he knew the pleasure of having a goal, a feeling that he hadn't known in months.

A film of perspiration chilled his skin as he left the workshop some hours later. His body ached, but he was satisfied, finally seeing the workbench emptied of rubbish and wiped clean. He would rest, eat something, and go back to the shop. He'd keep clearing away the past, with the hope of creating a new future.

Lorna Whiston's heart was pounding. The old woman's raptor nose was inches away. Her breath was sour. Her rheumy eyes held inexplicable hatred.

"I saw your little girl nicking those sweets, with me own eyes!" Old Miss Harrop's voice grew louder. "She ought to be disciplined!"

People gathered to watch the spectacle. Children who'd been playing on the green paused and stared intently. Lorna was thankful that, by now, Finley had probably gone along to his mate's house, and they lived north, on the other side of the pond. The old woman went on, shouting down the whole village. Lorna was about to walk away from the ugly encounter, but then she glanced at her daughter. Peony vined around Lorna's leg, her thumb plugged her mouth. Her little face was bathed in tears. All else forgotten, Lorna kneeled to talk the situation over with her daughter, ignoring the loud woman and whispering bystanders.

"Peony, did you take something from the shop?"

Peony opened her small fist and revealed a smashed piece of caramel wrapped in greaseproof paper. Lorna stood and turned on old Miss Harrop who continued with her enthusiastic indictment against Peony.

"Would you kindly stop, Miss Harrop?" Lorna tried to level her voice, controlling her volume, though she knew the old woman to be deaf as well as dumb. "She's only three and we're going back into the shop, now. She'll be made to apologise and return the sweet."

Lorna's memory darted back to a vivid scene. Miss Harrop, skinny, scary, and raven-like, was having a word with Lorna's mother outside the church. Lorna had been quite small at the time. When her mother came away from Miss Harrop, she was crying. Mona pulled her coat tighter around herself, as though Miss Harrop had given her a chill. Alarmed, Lorna had asked, "What's wrong, Mummy?"

Her mother had refused to tell her. She'd turned to Lorna and said in her soft voice, "That's a very unfriendly lady, and you're meant to stay away from her, alright?"

Lorna had been trying, rather unsuccessfully given the close perimeters of the village, to avoid Miss Harrop ever since. Despite Lorna's efforts, Peony had become the third generation of her family harangued by this odious woman.

"It's not just that, young lady," Miss Harrop barked. "I saw your brother this morning whilst driving in my car. Just like your father, he was, hobbling about. No doubt because of drink. And you? Them children of yourn, all of 'em by different fathers. What man haven't you had in the county, I'd like to know?"

A swift glance at her neighbours told Lorna they were embarrassed by Miss Harrop's comments. The pub owner's wife, Vicky, turned and walked away. A few others reverently followed her. Mrs. Pugh shook her head in disgust, as she and her two daughters passed quickly by, depriving Miss Harrop of the majority of her audience.

Miss Harrop seized little Peony by the shoulder. "You're a wicked child—"

Lorna's patience vanished. She freed her daughter from Miss Harrop's talon grip with one hand. With the other, she slapped the old woman's cheek.

A collective "Oh!" issued from the on-lookers.

Miss Harrop's gnarled fingers flew to her face. The old woman appeared too shocked to spew out one of her venomous retorts. Peony began to wail. There seemed little point in dragging her nearly hysterical child into Goodchild's to apologise. Lorna hoisted Peony onto her hip and left the high street, without so much as a backwards glance at the stunned Miss Harrop.

Walking towards her vehicle, Lorna's thinking was quite clear. She hadn't been muddled by old Miss Harrop. She hadn't been overcome by her emotions and thus "accidentally" acted out. Lorna had been perfectly lucid. She'd meant to hit the old cow; she'd meant to defend herself and family, to the point of risking what was left of her reputation, and perhaps being charged with assault.

Which, most unfortunately, was a distinct possibility.

With Peony strapped in her car seat and crying like a banshee, Lorna drove towards her friend's house, a tall, white, Victorian with a pair of bow windows, perched proudly at the top of the village, opposite the Twinns. She was meant to be going to Emily's after the shops anyway, to leave Peony before work.

Arriving at Emily's home, Lorna's hands trembled with nervous energy. Perhaps it was something to do with how she knew Emily would loyally take her side. Em always understood, even when Lorna acted badly.

And she certainly had acted *awfully* badly. Peony, who was recovering a bit, had stopped screaming, at least, in happy anticipation of visiting Emily and her baby. Lorna drove past Emily's detached house, with its bricked, front-garden wall that stood flush with the village road. She turned left, into a lane that came behind the row of houses and afforded parking space and a garage-en-bloc behind, where Emily's husband housed his unremarkable but reliable BMW saloon when he returned home from work.

Unloading Peony from her car seat, Lorna held her child close, instead of requiring that she walk. Peony's head dropped contentedly on Lorna's shoulder, as they made their way through the gate, and up the path through Emily's back garden. Emily had scarcely opened the door leading into the kitchen when Lorna launched into her retelling of the whole dreadful affair.

"Miss Harrop deserved something back in kind. You know she was disgraceful to my mother, even at Dad's funeral." Emily nodded her head in agreement. Lorna sat at her friend's kitchen table nursing a cuppa. Peony had stopped crying; Lorna had begun.

Emily's face was soft with compassion, holding her own little girl, her arms strong with the baby-muscles that young mothers develop from acting as human bounce chairs.

The Grahams–Emily with an older brother, David, and their parents–had lived over the road from the Whistons, and the girls were always together from the time they could toddle around the garden. Emily was a true friend, in spite of Lorna's frequently tumultuous circumstances. In contrast, Emily had a secure, calm life as Mrs. Henry Norcross. Pretty, quiet, demure Emily had married well, and her hard-working, computer programmer husband adored her and their baby girl, Bethany.

Lorna finished her story, and Emily said all of the right things to comfort her best mate. "But *you'd* never do such a thing," Lorna said.

Emily smiled. "No. But that doesn't mean I don't understand why you did."

Ever generous, Emily attempted to smooth over the old woman's behaviour, as well. "Lorna, you've got to wonder what it is that makes her so miserable—to be so unkind to our lovely Peony!" Peony heard her name and turned from playing on the rug to giggle at Emily.

"What's more," Lorna picked up her story again, "we were finally away, and as I turned the corner I plowed into that witch. She'll probably hex me, since she's certain to have heard all the fuss. Surely she and old Miss Harrop are in cahoots."

Emily chuckled and stood up, carrying Bethany to the shiny, recently refurbished worktop. "I almost forgot to offer you pudding. This turned out rather good, if I do say so myself." She sliced a piece of lemon cake one-handed, dropped it on a plate pulled from the rack, and passed it across the table.

"I don't miss Mum so much with you around, Em," Lorna said, quietly.

Emily returned to the table and gave Lorna's arm a squeeze. "And like a good mum I am going to remind you that you're due at the castle in 20 minutes, m'lady. You don't want to be a tardy chambermaid, I am sure."

"Hmm, don't. Leave me to get a sugar high in peace."

"She's not a witch, you know. She's rather nice."

"How do you know? Don't tell me you went into her shop? Or lair. Whatever."

Emily brought Bethany to rest on her shoulder. "It was rather odd, actually, but we met at the hairdressers in Stonewyck."

"Not so odd, given all those highlights in her hair. She looks like a model, towering above us all, with her spidery legs and slim hips. Adds to her witchiness."

"Lorna, honestly. She's lovely."

"But what does she *do*? More to the point, why is she *here*? She seems more suited to a posh place in London, than living at your parent's old cottage in our backwater. Are you sure she isn't wanted by the law?" Lorna's tummy fluttered as she thought, *Maybe the law wants me.*

Emily laughed. "I am quite sure she's completely respectable. She's a nutritional therapist, with more years training than a dietitian, but along the same lines. She has some sort of Oxbridge education, I can't remember exactly, but, I have to say, I am rather impressed with her. She suggested some diet changes for Bethany's rash, and it worked a treat."

"Yes, but the doctor—the *real* doctor—had already given you prescription cream, so how d'you know it wasn't already working?"

"It wasn't."

Lorna didn't answer back. Emily was all goodness, and there were times that you just felt like a sod if you gave her grief whilst she was defending someone's character. Sadly, Lorna took her last bite of cake, and asked, "What's her name?"

"Avalyn Smith."

"Avalyn? That's rather a nice name." Lorna sipped her tea. "I want to like it. But I can't."

Emily grinned. "No. Of course not."

Lorna took the M20 west towards Maidstone, and arrived at the castle with the windows down, whipping her hair into a mad frenzy. After talking with Emily, she felt calm and ready to work. She slowed and turned into a gated lane that meandered through the castle grounds, drove around a sweeping private drive, and parked behind the first of the holiday cottages. Lorna left her car windows down, and walked towards the first enormous cottage she would clean, which sometimes welcomed as many as ten guests. The house was one of six available to let, and, being several hundred years old, was one of the most delightfully antiquated. Her steps crushed the sweet alyssum which grew over the grassy car park in a wild purple profusion, and the trodden blooms released their strong honey scent. The clouds floated in front of the sun, shading the soft surface of the river into a bath of pewter. A gentle breeze teased the long tendrils of the chartreuse weeping willow trees lining the water. Through a break in the ancient trees, the stone castle stood solidly in the distance, with its black swans bobbing like toys on the moat.

Originally, Lorna had begun working as a cleaner up at the castle, before Finley was born. She'd been grateful to get a good paying job with benefits, a pension scheme, and insurance, and her boss was most gracious about the time she took away when Finley arrived. While Emily watched over her baby boy, Lorna worked the day visitor route, cleaning her way through the cavernous castle.

New on staff, Lorna had been responsible for the gloomiest areas of the ancient fortress. She had cleaned miles of medieval stone flooring, dusting and polishing around casks in the cellar, as well as creepy suits of armour circa 1640. She enjoyed a bit of history as well as the next person, but sometimes her imagination got away from her. Up a rippled flight of stone steps was an imposing suit of armour stood on a high pedestal, a sharp spotlight glinting off the metal. Lorna had to unlock the barred gate behind which the knight stood, towering above her on his platform. She dusted his feet, clearing a cobweb between the dampish castle wall and the armour, sending a spider scuttling into the dark alcove behind. She dreaded having to work her way up his imposing stature, with her long-handled duster. Noticing a particular dent in the armour's chest—could it have been from a strike during battle? Was it a fatal blow? —and daydreaming about how terrifying it would have been to be in the castle under siege, Lorna glanced up at the knight and saw a pair of eyes bearing down at her, shining from the slit in the knight's helmet.

She gasped and ran down the passage, forgetting to pull the alcove gate shut. Feigning a headache, she'd begged a co-worker to go and lock the knight into his niche. She'd forced herself to return and clean there again, but she worked quickly and listened to music, and never looked at his face when she was behind the iron-gate with him.

Although her own actions embarrassed her, even in secret, some days she just couldn't risk the scary fancies that caused a tickle to run down her spine, so she cowardly skipped her dusting duties in the alcove where the armour stood, armed and ready to strike her dead. She imagined the news headlines: "Mother of Two Murdered, Blood Found on Medieval Knight's Sword."

Perhaps even worse was the way Henry VIII's portrait eyes followed her progress at the end of the day when she silently paced across the ebony wood floor of the ornate Banquetting Hall. Very fitting, Lorna always thought, as the man obviously had had a tremendous appetite. Proving herself an otherwise industrious employee for several years, she confidently applied for, and received, a new position at the holiday cottages nearly four years ago, a few days before learning she was pregnant with Peony.

It was a great job, as Lorna was keen to work on her own and then enjoyed meeting up with her mates at teatime. She thrived on her responsibilities, relished tidying up the beautiful houses with their lovely exposed beams, beautifully appointed furnishings, and private gardens. She took pride in refreshing bouquets of flowers for the next guests, wiping fine dust from the diamond-paned leaded windows, and hovering non-existent soil from the thick carpets. The tourists, able to afford the luxury prices the castle charged, tended to use the accommodations gently, but occasionally she found children's messes of crumbs, smudgy handprints on the glass garden door, and smelly nappies left behind in an open dustbin, leaving an aroma strong enough to choke a horse after being shut up inside the cottage during a long, hot summer morning.

She was about to finish the rambling Loidis Cottage when her mobile rang. The incoming numbers signified a call from the castle's office. "Hello, this is Lorna. May I help?"

"Lorna, it's Iona, from human resources. Would you mind to stop before leaving today? I have a bit of news I need to share with you."

"Of course, Iona. See you this afternoon."

Lorna rang off, her heart in a wild skip. Iona was a gruff Scotswoman, and her tone always made Lorna feel a bit like she'd been caught being naughty. But surely if the police had been tracking Lorna down for her violence on old Miss Harrop then Iona would ask to see her immediately. It wasn't the time of year to have a meeting about getting a rise or discussing performance. Iona wouldn't have anything pleasant to say.

Chapter Three

"OKAY MATE, YOU mustn't tell your Mum, as we're doing something quite dangerous. Are you ready?"

Finley grinned, pumping his head up and down. He'd surprised his uncle by following him, puppy-like, into Oakley Whiston's old garage workshop.

"We've not been allowed in here, you know," Finley said. "Mum says its full of old junk and we could get a cut and our jaws would clamp shut and then we'd die."

"Sounds rather serious. No deep, bloody gashes allowed, then." They laughed. Simon took boyish pleasure in usurping Lorna's rules. It was rather discomforting that this was the best fun he'd had in a long while.

Simon dragged a tall ladder from where it leaned against a wall. "Alright, listen carefully. I'll put the clean rag on, secure it with an elastic band, and pass the broom up to you. Run it 'round the light fixture above you. Cautiously, Fin. Should you start to come off, I'll catch you."

He sent Finley up the folding stairs and then supplied his nephew with clean cloth. Simon coughed as clumps of dirt fell from the angled broom in Finley's hand, but he daren't leave his position at the bottom of the ladder. Better filthy and safe, rather than clean and sorry.

"That's a fine job, Bob," Simon said, rhyming his compliment to make Finley smile as he descended the ladder. The boy was proud of following instructions and keen to clean the other light fixtures.

"Speaking of, what do I get paid for this?"

"Cheeky monkey. Didn't your Mum tell you how penniless I am? You ought instead to be thinking how we're going to hide these clothes. They'll be dirty enough to warrant burning when we're through." Finley was doing his nine year-old best to help Simon manage the ladder and bring it under the next light.

Finley, now an old pro, scrambled up the ladder. There was less confidence in his voice, though, when he asked, "Is it true that you were married to a French lady?"

Not a question Simon expected, but, on the other hand, it was hard to imagine what his impetuous sister may have said. "Yes, it's true. She was called Dominique. She was beautiful and very clever, too. Her job was to visit businesses and see what sort of artwork was needed to advertise their business. Then she'd come back to the place she worked, and tell the artist what to do up. Dominique was brilliant at matching art to businesses, to help them have an identity and to sell their wares or services. It's called marketing."

Capable and on task, Finley never stopped working as he listened. "It's good the way you keep your hands moving, Fin, instead of pausing to chat like most lads. That's getting the work done."

Finley wore an irrepressible smile as he came down the ladder. He stood for a moment on the hard concrete, absently wiping his grimy hands on his jeans. "Did she do art things for you? I mean, when you made furniture?"

"Oh, so you've worked out how I met her," Simon replied with a laugh. "Yes, she did. Dominique asked me lots of questions. She was learning something about the kind of furniture we made, you see? Then, off she went. Next thing I knew, she came back 'round with a nice logo. It was the business name with scarlet and black lines around the letters, and a tag line, to tell people what we do. 'Whiston's Hand Crafted Furniture, *Tomorrow's Heirlooms,*

Traditionally Hand Made Today.' She arranged for a sign to be made and put up outside the workshop. And of course, she was right on point with everything else, too. A website design, and business cards done up, and the like."

They moved to the final light fixture. "Then what happened?"

"Well, a lot." This time, Fin stopped working to listen. "The business was a success. I was working all the time. Never took a holiday. Then a rather odd thing happened, I started having a lot of pain in my body. On top of that, there was a bloke who caught me out, Fin."

The boy came slowly down the ladder, eager for the climax of the story. He waited, eyes wide and staring, for his uncle to continue.

"I couldn't do some of the trickier hand crafting anymore. The pain was getting worse. My hands weren't working for me, you see. The furniture was dear because each piece took a lot of hours and care. Each range was rather special and expensive. But to keep up with orders, I began cutting corners, buying some pre-cut wood and so on. Although the furniture were still 95 percent made by hand, 'mostly handcrafted' isn't quite the same, is it? An important customer found me out, called me a fraud, even took me to court. The business suffered. By then, my health problems worsened. I could scarcely walk."

"Paying the legal fees and settlement—the bloke who sold our furniture in his upscale shop, the one who brought action against me, won the lawsuit, you see—wiped out my bank account, savings, and my retirement. I even had to sell equipment, not only in the workshop, but in the office, too." Simon sighed, and ran his hand around his chin. They stood for a moment, each of them thinking.

"As it happens, my wife was rather weary of everything. She wanted a divorce. I didn't argue with her. I even gave her the house and one of my better earning investments, and I kept the debt. She didn't deserve to suffer for what I'd done, right?"

Finley nodded. "I didn't think you'd tell me, but I am glad you did."

"Maybe I shouldn't have told you, Fin. But I remember thinking when I was your age that adults were rather off the mark when it came to children. You lot understand much more than we'd like to give you credit for, isn't that right?"

"Yeah."

The calendar turned to September. The early autumn sun retained warmth through most of the day, but the evenings were stealing in earlier. Long shadows engulfed Simon as he sat at a picnic table in the side garden by the house, gazing at the workshop. He leaned forward, his elbows on the old, grey, wooden tabletop, his ankles crossed beneath him. A mug of tea stood on the table before him, forgotten and cold. His mind was full of plans for the future. Simon imagined feeling better, going back to creating furniture or at least something rendered in wood. His dad's old workshop would work a treat. He could begin again, maybe by taking orders to restore fine antiques, mending old pieces.

When he was last driving through the village, he'd noticed there was nowhere for people to rest on the edge of the green. He'd had an inspiration to build a garden bench or two to be placed there. If Simon's health improved, perhaps he could help the vicar as well. When he'd brought the children to church last Sunday, he saw the pews were in want of refinishing.

Strokes of charcoal were colouring over the radiant pink and orange tinged sunset as Simon allowed his fantasy to wander a little further afield. After making a bit of money, there were some larger projects to tackle. Perhaps expanding the farmhouse for Lorna. Building his own home, here on the family's land. There was an ideal site on the other side of the workshop, up on the knoll, overlooking the beautiful countryside, with a view of patchwork fields rising up to the distant ridge. Upstairs in his imagined dream house, he knew he'd be able to glimpse a bit of the village church spire, and a corner of the green; that'd be the best place for the master bedroom. He began a mental list of the men he would hire on to do the plumbing, electrical and so on, savouring the most appealing part of the plan for his own home: fitted bookshelves, a hand built staircase, and, of course, the furniture.

His reverie was interrupted when Lorna came outside, and he

was surprised she'd sought him out. Clouds had closed across the sky like sitting room curtains, drawn to shut out the night. Lorna's arms were folded across her chest, her chin tucked down. "It's gotten colder," he said, suddenly feeling the chill of the oncoming darkness. He noticed that she sat down gently on the bench beside him, aware that jostling him may cause him pain.

"I've really only just arrived, but I'll miss Finley when the school term starts."

"He loves having you here, and I think it's good for him."

The statement was especially generous coming from his sister. He'd missed his wife, but he had also missed not having any family. "Finley's good for me, too."

"I made an arse of myself today," Lorna said, raising her hands to make a ponytail of her hair, then dropping it. "At the time, I thought I had good reason. But now, I feel dreadful."

"What happened?"

"That old cow, Miss Harrop. She saw Peony nick a sweet in Goodchild's. She shouted us down in the street."

"And?"

"I slapped her. Rather hard, I am sorry to say. It's a wonder she didn't go reeling."

"Good heavens!"

"You said that just like Mum." Her smile faded. "Which makes me feel worse. I don't know why a prim and proper woman like Mum was cursed with a daughter like me. I could've been arrested, Simon. In fact, Miss Harrop might still bring charges against me. Half the village could stand as witnesses."

Simon slipped his arm around his sister's shoulders. "Dear old dad contributed to your DNA, which explains a lot, doesn't it. But we're determined to rise above, yes?"

"Most definitely." She turned to him. "But that's why this is quite serious," Lorna's voice wavered and she wiped away a tear. "Because I want my kids to be good people. And there I was, smacking an old woman in the street. It hadn't even bothered me till I got to Em's. It's not like I was in a rage. I knew what I was about, and simply didn't care. Do you think I am some sort of psychotic?"

"No, love. Just a young mother, with rather a lot on her shoulders, and perhaps a bit of a short fuse. What are you going to do about it?"

"What can I do?"

"Showing Peony how to apologise, mightn't that be a start?"

"How can I do that, Simon? It'll be difficult as it is, showing my face in the village. There were people gathering. Miss Harrop's crony —that little mousy woman, I've forgotten what she's called—and the entire Coombes family—I acted as though I was a woman possessed in front of their triplets as well. Even that witchy woman was lurking about. Not to mention, I am still meant to drag Peony back into the shop to apologise to Molly, and pay for the sweet."

"You could go 'round to Miss Harrop's house?"

Lorna thought for a moment about her brother's suggestion. "I don't know, Simon."

"Surely you don't believe as we did when we were kids."

"Of course not, but her gate always looks so foreboding, and I've never heard of anyone going in there, even Ernie. She still picks up her post in the village, instead of him delivering. I've no idea why, except that she seems to despise visitors."

They said nothing more for a few minutes.

"You're quite right," Lorna said decisively. "I'll go tomorrow. I'll try to see her at home. But I shan't take Peony with me, just in case it's a mistake."

She couldn't bear to give him the rest of her news.

Chapter Four

EACH MEMBER OF this family would rather spend the morning in any other way, thought Simon. He was off to his job interview for a position teaching a woodworking course at the community college. Finley was returning to the village primary school for the autumn term. Lorna was venturing to old Miss Harrop's, after taking Peony to Emily's so that she could apologise to the old bat on her own.

If Simon was taken on it would mean a long commute, but he would be glad to have work, no matter what the pay, inconvenience, or the pain that came with a considerable drive. Close to the campus now, he came to a traffic light and took a long sip of cola.

Perhaps there weren't any other applicants, in which case there was no cause for worry; merely showing up and being adequately qualified would be enough. When Simon operated his business, he only took on skilled craftsman, always keen to find people who knew even more than he about constructing high quality furniture. He had a lot of knowledge on the offer—much more, in fact, than the course required, since it was meant to be an introduction to carpentry and the rudiments of joining wood, as well as learning the basics of hand tools and portable power tools. At the conclusion, the students would take a written exam, and complete a simple project.

The traffic light turned green and he drove through, turning left into the college car park. He'd come a little early so as to have enough time to ease himself out of the van and work some of the stiffness out of his joints before meeting up with a man called Harvey.

After a brief stretch and a look about, he located the correct building and went inside. The door closed behind him, blocking out the light and bathing him in the cold, blue, artificial light of the hallway. It had been a long time—since he was sixteen, in fact—since he'd been inside a school. He walked to the end of the hall, turned right, and came to a door marked as the carpentry shop. Not sure whether to knock or simply walk in, Simon decided to do both, rapping on the door and then a moment later, opening it. To his relief, there was only one person inside, a man at the far end of a shop-like classroom. The man looked up and began walking towards Simon.

Simon put on his best smile, and shook hands with Mr. Harvey.

"I recognise your name, Mr. Whiston," Harvey said, having gotten through the formalities.

"Oh, I see." Simon didn't, really. He wasn't exactly sure where Harvey might be taking the conversation.

"Your reputation as a fine furniture maker is impressive. Rest assured, I am more interested in the immense talent that brought you up to having a workshop on Regent Street, and selling at the top of the market, rather than having an interest in your reasons for, ah, *retiring* from business."

"I appreciate that, Mr. Harvey. People are quick to throw stones these days."

"Certainly. Now, I require all of my teacher applicants to demonstrate their ability with a brief and simple exercise in the desired subject. In this case, I ask that you would please produce a mortise and tenon joint with these pieces of wood using the hand tools." Mr. Harvey paused, no doubt remembering reports of Simon Whiston's famous failure to use traditional hand tools. "Naturally, you're meant to walk me through the process, as though you were teaching a student. You'll have eight minutes."

"Yes, of course," Simon said, smiling again, this time to infuse himself with confidence. He coerced his limbs to move with ease towards the workbench. Harvey's assignment was a basic technique he'd done thousands of times, hand cutting and squaring a piece of wood to be fitted in a square socket. He picked up an appropriate sized chisel, explaining to his faux student that the width of the chisel determines the width that the joint will become. He bought a few moments to rest his fingers while explaining to Harvey how to mark the tenon, pressing the gauge against the face of the wood each time.

Tiny shards of fire and glass surged through his fingers as he scored the wood. Resisting the urge to ball his throbbing fingers into fists, Simon clamped the wood in the vise, securing it for cutting. The vise was old and didn't spin easily, and Simon grew warm from the effort. He took a deep breath and picked up a small brass-backed dovetail saw. Simon cut out the centre of the tenon, cheeks then shoulders. Although the physical work was demanding, Simon knew he did a fine job instructing. Forcing his hands to obey the innate skill he'd mastered over years, Simon carefully held a chisel, pounding it with a mallet, chipping out the square that would hold the tenon in a perfectly fitted embrace.

"Almost finished," Simon announced with too much evident relief. But quite suddenly, the pain in his hands traveled a hot, quick track up into both his wrists. He attempted to put the chisel against the wood, to pry the chippings out of the indentation he'd made, but his fingers wouldn't take hold. His explanation of the technique went lifeless and eventually mute.

Mr. Harvey shifted his weight from one foot to another. An eternity passed and finally Simon went back to hitting the chisel with the mallet, but it was quite obvious that he'd come to the end of himself.

"Well, it's mostly done, that," Simon mumbled, looking with intensity at the wood, willing it to somehow have clean edges, so that he could satisfactorily join the pieces. Not unlike how he longed for his life to properly join up again.

He knew that he ought to shake Mr. Harvey's hand, but that

wasn't about to happen, either, lest Simon begin crying like a little girl.

Desperately, he wrung his aching hands as he apologised to Mr. Harvey. Simon couldn't meet his eyes, as he abruptly turned and fled the interview.

Lorna pulled her car onto the shallow drive at Miss Harrop's until her bumper nearly tapped the formidable, steel gate. A chain and lock circled the top rail, rusting but still securely marrying the gate to the post. There must be another way onto the property since old Miss Harrop drove a car. Lorna didn't have the patience to search for another entrance and left her vehicle at the impassable gate.

She mounted the tall gate to go over the top. She paused for a moment, straddling, looking from her perch for signs of movement at the house, but there were none. She completed her climb and strode purposefully up the grassy drive, rehearsing her apology speech. Lorna hadn't seen Miss Harrop since the incident, a relief, as she'd had to make a stop in the village yesterday. She planned to make this a very short visit indeed, expecting Miss Harrop to be nearly impossible to apologise to, and, as well, she had a busy day and needed to get on.

Lorna knocked on a door that could've done with a lick of paint. Noticing the disrepair calmed her nerves a bit. No response. Lorna knocked again, this time following up her sore knuckles with a bit of a kick to the bottom of the door, just to be certain she was heard. She looked around. The garden had gone to seed. Knee-high grass waved round the edges of an area where gravel had been thrown down. Impatiently, Lorna peeked into the window left of the front door, but it was blocked by a filmy sheer, and something dark.

Perhaps Miss Harrop was around the back of the house, pegging out laundry or something. Disappointment made her irritated. She despised the notion of seeing old Miss Harrop in the village, for God only knew what would happen. Without further deliberation, she rounded the house. A wind chime tinkled her arrival, but otherwise there wasn't any movement or civilised sound.

The back door rattled loosely beneath Lorna's fist as she gave it a swift pound. Her hand found the doorknob and turned it. Impetuous, that's what Simon always said of her. Well, if he could see her now.

The door opened easily. Lorna called out, nearly failing to leave off the "old" when she sang out a greeting to Miss Harrop. She peered around the door into the kitchen. That's when she saw the old lady on the filthy, grey linoleum floor in front of a dark green Aga, with a mournful looking marmalade cat sitting watch beside her.

"Miss Harrop?"

Lorna flung open the door and stopped, not entirely sure if she wanted to come closer should the woman actually be dead. Well trained in scenting out odd smells before making loathsome discoveries—a proficiency that served experienced housekeepers well—Lorna employed a deep sniff. The room didn't smell like death. Although it did reek of fish and mold.

Slowly, she approached the body on the floor. The cat gave out a deep, loud meow, giving Lorna a start. She knelt beside Miss Harrop. Her courage failed and she looked around the kitchen for a moment. Then she forced herself to reach out and grasp Miss Harrop's wrist, feeling for a pulse. The old woman groaned and turned her head, but didn't open her eyes. Lorna was happy to let go of the flaccid limb and edge away.

She dug into her large handbag, seized upon her mobile, and dialed 999. She gave Miss Harrop's address, and tried to answer the questions of the dispatch person, who seemed to suss out rather quickly that Lorna was clueless.

"Miss Harrop?" Lorna said, probably a bit overly loud.

The old woman's eyes rolled open, zig-zagged and then rested on Lorna's face. "*You!*"

"I came by to apologise to you, Miss Harrop. I've called for help. They'll be here soon to look after you."

The old woman stared blankly at the ceiling. Miss Harrop's face, devoid of its usual hateful expression, made her look like an altogether different person and made it easier to be kind.

"Don't worry, Miss Harrop."

She thought about going to move her car, but she felt rather odd leaving the woman lying on the floor. Anyway, there was so little room in front of the gate that she couldn't imagine it would make a difference. The people coming on the ambulance would ask her more questions, but she didn't know how she could possibly add to what had already been said on the phone—nothing of any assistance whatsoever. Like it or not, she was caught up in the drama of the situation and wasn't about to drive off and go about her day not knowing what had transpired. She'd just have to wait and accept the fact that she was useless. Somehow, she was becoming a little accustomed to the horrid stench of the house.

Miss Harrop drifted off to sleep. Lorna backed herself into a chair at the kitchen table some three feet away.

The minutes passed slowly.

Lorna got a message from Emily. *How did it go?* She didn't bother to respond, as there was too much to relate. Wouldn't Em be surprised with this turn of events!

There was knocking at the front door, and Lorna realised hadn't said anything to the dispatcher about coming into the back door. *Silly as pie am I*, she thought, realising that she could now just open the door from inside the house. As she stood she noticed the cat watching her, the loyal fellow hadn't moved from his post. Lorna turned the corner to go through to the front sitting room.

Two steps from the kitchen were as far as she got. There'd been no one walking through to the front room for *quite* some time.

The room was stacked to the rafters with…*stuff*. It was incredible.

"Come 'round to the back, please." She heard a muffled response.

Turning towards the back garden, she stepped gingerly around Miss Harrop, whom she hoped hadn't expired, and opened the door wide. Fresh country air was a good thing. Two uniformed men were just rounding the corner.

"Hello, love, you rang in about an old lady, did you? A neighbour, you are, isn't that what you told our Lucy?"

"Yes," Lorna said to the gentleman, who was truly gentle. "She's here, in the kitchen. I've no idea what's wrong with her," Lorna said. "Or," remembering some of the questions put to her over the phone, "her medical history, or anything about her family. I am sorry I can't be of more help."

"No worries, love," said the kindly medic, stepping confidently into the house. Lorna half expected him to whistle while we worked.

She looked on as the men took Miss Harrop's pulse, listened to her heart, attempted to speak with her. The grey-templed gentleman said to his younger, quiet associate, "A bit dehydrated."

"How do y'know that?" Lorna blurted, intrigued.

The medic turned and answered, "Her skin's looser than it should be, love. See how it comes away when we give a bit of a pinch? We'll be taking her to hospital. She'll probably be just fine, don't you worry."

"Alright." She watched as they pulled a safety belt securely around the old woman's body, and then lifted Miss Harrop, who seemed to weigh very little, on a black ambulance stretcher. Lorna backed up, and bumped into the kitchen table. Turning around self-consciously, to give the table a nasty look for being in the way, she saw Miss Harrop's handbag.

"Oh, look. Her bag may have her information in it."

The younger man retrieved the handbag from Lorna. "Yes, quite helpful Miss, thank you."

The men left, trundling through the back garden, carrying Miss Harrop on the frame, and disappeared around the corner of the house. Lorna spared a thought for the cat, and went to see that it had been fed and watered.

She found the cat's dishes close-by, and they were full of water and dry food. Perhaps Miss Harrop had been feeling well this morning, or perhaps the cat was a good hunter and only ate from his dish occasionally.

Feeling rather low, she decided to sit for a moment, and then decided against it when she looked again at the state of the table. Something sticky had congealed close to where she'd rested her arm whilst looking at her mobile. *Eww.*

Lorna resettled her handbag on her shoulder, crossed her arms and surveyed the kitchen with care. Clearly, it was filthy. The items stacked up on the cupboard—the newspapers, plastic tubs, envelopes and so on—had been collecting for ages. Maybe years. She summoned her courage and made her way again towards the front sitting room. Masses of rubbish filled the room, rug to rafter, creating a shapeless, overwhelming dump. It was nearly impossible to tell what was what.

Lorna turned and started down the passage towards the bedrooms and the loo. She stopped in the dark hall.

Bad smells.

She felt a pressing need to escape into the sunshine of Miss Harrop's overgrown garden.

Chapter Five

AVALYN SMITH FINISHED her virtual duties. Modern technology meant that she could consult with her established patients online, answering simple questions, renewing assessments and updating care plans, all from her office in the village. It had been a good source of income, too, as she built up her new clientele in Burleigh Cross and the surrounding area.

Or, rather, didn't build up her new clientele.

She was none too popular, and she'd heard whispering over her shoulder when she did a bit of shopping, passed local people on the footpath, or attempted to be friendly. People were kind enough, but they didn't understand the role of a nutritional therapist. They were pleased enough to see their GP, Doctor Clewely, when he could finally squeeze them into his surgery schedule in a neighbouring village. He was responsible for visiting several offices in Kent, and Avalyn knew there were many health complaints with which she could help if only she were given a chance.

She turned off her computer, and drained the rest of her coffee. Taking the mug and a plate littered with dry muffin crumbs, she made her way to the small kitchenette at the back of her office, and did the washing up. She watered the avocado plant, a science experiment with a friend's child, to see if it was really true that you could push the fruit's stone into soil and acquire a not-so-lovely houseplant. Avalyn smiled every time she looked at the remnant of a guacamole recipe which had given way to lovely green shoots, standing up to catch the sun in the tiny kitchen window that faced the village green.

She extinguished the lights in the hallway and front of the office, and locked the door behind her. Smiling and waving goodbye to Molly through the window of Goodchild's shop, Avalyn rounded the building to the mews car park, and settled into her tiny car for the short drive home. The simple act of being acknowledged by some friendly person, at some point during the day, had meant more to Avalyn than Molly could possibly know. Someone had once said, in a movie that had made Avalyn cry, that we all need witnesses to our lives, someone to notice that we're here and participating in life on the planet. Molly was one of the few people in Avalyn's daily routine who may be aware if Avalyn had come to work on time in the morning, if she nipped home for lunch or ate in, or if she had left the office late because she had lost track of the hour while working on her computer.

In the months since she'd arrived, Avalyn's only close friend was her great white dog, and he was perhaps more a liability than his dedicated companionship was worth. A cross between an Alsatian and a Great Pyrenees, Gus embodied the negatives of both breeds. Led by his nose and a will to herd or hunt, he was ever playing the Houdini, freeing himself of every restriction she placed upon him, and generally running amok. No amount of walking seemed to tire him, no change in diet or giving him a generously sized dog run seemed to entice him to stay at home. It was rather like he was set on being rid of her, perhaps a bit like the inhabitants of Burleigh Cross.

This had not been his strategy at the adoption centre, of course. When Avalyn first saw Gus, he pleaded with his large dark eyes for her to rescue him. There wasn't a shred of evidence that he was anything but an intelligent, loyal, guard-dog sort of chap. She settled on him immediately without a thought that he'd turned her plum-coloured trench into a coat resembling his own, or that he would cost nearly the same as feeding a horse. Gus's adoption was a bit out of line with Avalyn Smith's character, as was leaving London and striking out into the wilds of Kent.

Avalyn parked her vehicle beside the door of the cottage that she let from the Graham's. She knew Gus had kept to his run in the back garden, from the sound of his heavy tail whacking a greeting against the wooden fence. Instead of going to Gus, she set about on a special errand. She wasn't quite sure of herself, but she intended to pay a call on Lorna Whiston. Perhaps it was because Lorna was her closest neighbour, or perhaps Avalyn felt a bit reassured by the obvious fact that Lorna wasn't bothered overly much by social conventions. She'd seen Lorna and her little girl being shouted at by old Miss Harrop. Avalyn had flinched when Lorna struck the old woman. It was rather an off-putting scene, but as Avalyn herself had already suffered repercussions from Miss Harrop's vicious tongue, she could well imagine what years of that sort of animosity had inspired in Lorna Whiston.

Avalyn paused at the curve of the road, studying the Whiston's farmhouse. She knew that Lorna was usually at home on Thursdays, and, in fact, her vehicle was parked in the drive. Avalyn stood on the edge of the lane, rooted to the spot. People had always assumed her to be confident. She could understand how her appearance created that impression; she was tall, thin, reasonably poised and educated well enough that she ought to have something intelligent to say. But the truth was, she was rather shy. And she found that social settings were quite different to work. Avalyn found it much easier to listen to people's problems and offer clinical solutions than to approach them on a personal basis.

Particularly as she was seeking a favour and might be rebuffed.

A shiver of trepidation passed through her. She recalled the sharp look on Lorna Whiston's face as she had retreated, devil may care, from the shocked Miss Harrop. But what had Avalyn to lose, considering her total absence of friends, clients, or any sort of social standing? She forced herself to buck up and walk towards the farmhouse.

Lorna answered the door so quickly that Avalyn was taken aback.

"Yes?"

"Oh, hello." Avalyn felt suddenly quite embarrassed. What had she been thinking?

"I am Avalyn Smith. Your neighbour from Hawk's Nest Cottage, across the way, there." Avalyn usefully pointed out the only other house within a quarter of a mile.

"Uh-huh."

Not exactly the warm greeting she'd hoped for. Avalyn stumbled on. "It would seem that you have quite a lot of space here. Acreage, as it were. And, well, I wondered, if you'd consider allowing me to let a small bit of it. I want to plant a garden, you see, and I know it's rather late in the year and everything, but..." She'd run out of momentum and willed Lorna to say something.

"Won't you step in?" Lorna didn't smile, but she held the door open wide.

"Yes, certainly. Thank you," Avalyn's voice quaked. No doubt, Lorna must think of her as a nervous Nelly.

"Cup of tea?" Lorna began filling the kettle.

"Yes, please."

Clutching her handbag—why had she brought it? —Avalyn drew in a deep breath and told herself that this was actually going rather well. She hadn't been told to clear off. And she certainly hadn't expected to be given tea. Being asked in was quite remarkable. It was the first home she'd been invited into, since moving to Burleigh Cross.

"You can sit down, you know," Lorna snipped, taking a seat at the table. "I've heard good things about you, probably from the only person in our loving little village who would own up to having anything good to say."

Lorna's bluntness didn't offend her; her statement had been simply spoken, free of malice, and Avalyn knew that it was true. She'd only treated several dozen patients since arriving. The majority of them came from other villages, eager to slip into her office unobserved by anyone they knew. Somehow, she'd ended up in the deepest backwater in the entire country when it came to their outlook on nutritional therapy.

"And which of my two clients...?"

Lorna gratified Avalyn with a wide grin. "My best mate, Emily Norcross. You treated her baby for rash. Emily said you thought it was milk allergy, and you were right. I understand from Em that although it's a common condition, it's one that GPs often overlook."

"Oh, yes, of course. What a lovely little girl Bethany is, and Emily was kind to ring and say that Bethany's skin has cleared since she's been avoiding dairy." Avalyn relaxed. "Where is your little girl today?"

"She's with Emily, whose cousin has a daughter Peony's age and they adore playing together, so Emily takes Peony along and the little girls entertain themselves so Em and her cousin can have a proper chat. And my son, Finley, has returned to school for the autumn term, and will be playing with his friends after. I had a call to make earlier, and I didn't want to take Peony with me."

With this statement, Lorna grew silent. Her shoulders visibly slumped. Avalyn often saw this change in posture with her patients. They'd come into her surgery, seemingly carefree, until it was time to come to the point. As soon as they spoke of their malaise, their shoulders would droop, or perhaps they'd no longer be able to meet her eyes, as if they were ashamed of their health issue. Lorna swung her knees from under the table, shoved herself to her feet, brought the tea, milk, and sugar to the table, and pushed an opened tin towards her guest. There were three stale looking biscuits within, nestled deep in crumbs. Avalyn took a swig of the black, steaming tea for courage.

"Sorry to pry, but I wonder if something is bothering you?" There, she'd done it. She'd been too forward and probably would be asked to leave, regardless of tea having been served.

Lorna's chin shot up, her eyes shifting back and forth, bearing into Avalyn's. It was a bit distressing, but Avalyn didn't look away. It was a sort of test, Lorna's eyes seeking something in her own, and she was determined to pass muster. Surely, the woman didn't go round striking people routinely. Just in case, Avalyn steeled herself in her chair.

But all that issued from Lorna Whiston was a defeated sigh.

"It's been a dreadful day," Lorna said, pursing her lips together. "We won't pretend you don't know about my row with old Miss Harrop, will we? This morning I'd gone to her house, to apologise. Something I didn't relish doing in the middle of Goodchild's or on the village green."

Lorna paused in her story to take some tea, glancing at her neighbour. Avalyn nodded, showing quiet support.

"That funny old stick has this ridiculous sort of gate across her drive, so I had to leave the car in front of it, and climb over and walk some distance to the house." Lorna leaned back in her chair and shook her head in fresh disbelief. "I found her lying on the kitchen floor. She hadn't answered my knock, and, I don't know, I just wandered about. The back door was open, and there she was. I rang the ambulance service."

"How distressing for you."

"No, that's not it. Not to say that that part wasn't a bit scary at first, because I imagined she might be dead. The medic said she'd be right as rain, she was only dehydrated, or something simple. *It was what came after.*"

Avalyn recognised the moment. Lorna was about to share a confidence. However unlikely, they were sort of friends now, united by Lorna's story.

"The kitchen was far from tidy, mind you, but then I went through to the sitting room. The ambulance people were knocking at the front door, you see. And it was all hoarded in there."

"What do you mean?"

"I mean, I've never seen such a tip in my life. Newspapers, old coveralls that looked as though some farmer wore them centuries ago, electrical wire, broken crockery, bits of paper and even a big pile of those plastic sleeves that bread comes in. I've seen that sort of thing on TV, but never in real life. I wonder if that's what made her ill?"

"Doubtful. She's probably lived like that for years. You'd never know it to look at her. She always seems clean and pressed, doesn't she?"

"Yes," Lorna agreed. "Cruel, but tidy. I started down the passage towards the loo and her bedrooms, but got frightened of what I might discover. The stench was awful."

"How dreadful."

"The question is, what's to be done about it? I'd spend my time helping her to clear it out, but I can't afford to hire a skip to take it all away." Lorna brought her elbows to the table and leaned over, as though weighted by Miss Harrop's problem. "And perhaps she wouldn't want help, but it seems I ought to do something. Go to the council, or a magistrate? Or maybe even report it to the police? If she comes home from hospital with a visiting nurse, someone might try and take her home away, don't you think?"

"Well, clinically speaking, hoarding has only just recently been recognised as a disorder, and as such, she could get help if her doctor is made aware. Although, statistically, most people don't respond to treatment, so you mustn't get your hopes high that Miss Harrop will come along and willingly let you clear it all away. But you're quite right about all the legal issues; it's possible that she's broken health codes. If you're asking my opinion, it seems best to notify her family."

"I don't know who that would be. Presumably she has family, but none that I've ever heard of. No one's been on that property in donkey's years, excepting herself, and she might have shown me right off had she not been more or less unconscious." Lorna pushed back her chair. "I've got to collect Peony shortly. Let's take a walk and see which area suits for your garden."

Finley found him in the workshop.

"What's news, Master Finley?"

"You've got to come in now because I am nearly starved, and supper's almost ready."

"I've only got to put these cartons over here. What's your Mum heated up for our dining pleasure?"

"Something out of a box, I expect. Smelled like sausage rolls and chips. She did the shopping today, so there's a new tin of biscuits with some chocolate on them."

Simon didn't eat much these days. Discontinuing his medication hadn't really brought back his appetite. If he had a decent breakfast, soda would do the rest of the day.

"Your Gran did these fry ups in the morning that would cause Ernie the postman to come right to the door hoping for an invite to breakfast. She made bread, and all sorts of puddings that people would request every time there was a do at the church. She was a brilliant cook."

"And Mum's not," replied Finley, sharing a laugh with his uncle.

The Whiston family sat down to their meal, folded their hands, and bowed their heads. Gemma Giraffe prayed, "For our food about to eat, God and us be too-ly thankful."

"Peony, you'll have to put Gemma on your lap now." Lorna cut Peony's sausage roll into small pieces.

"It was a good day," Finley said, to no one in particular. Lorna shared a smile with her brother as Finley contemplated his plate.

"What made it so?" Simon responded.

"Football. In fact, coach says I am a natural. I am thinking of going professional."

It was Lorna's turn to look at her food, and Simon stifled a chuckle. "I can say I knew you when. And what club do you intend to play for, I wonder?"

"Now you're winding me up, Uncle Simon," Finley paused, chewing. "But since you asked, I wouldn't exactly turn down Liverpool, if they offered me more than Manchester."

"Sound thinking, our Finley."

Lorna looked at Simon. "And what about you? How'd your job interview come off at the college?"

Simon cleared his throat and wished his sister hadn't asked him in front of the children. He'd wanted them to feel secure now that he was living here. Yet, all he'd actually managed was using the last of his savings to chip in for groceries, and wasting copious amounts of fuel driving to job interviews.

"I don't think Mr. Harvey thought I was the top candidate. Unfortunately, I didn't tell him that Fin would soon be famous and he'd regret not having me on staff."

Finley laughed, joined by Peony, who inspired Gemma the Giraffe to give out a girly, high-pitched "moo."

"Mum, can I eat my chips on the floor while I watch my show?"

"Me, too," Peony chimed in.

The children were given permission to leave the table.

"I am sorry, Simon."

"Something'll turn up, Sis, don't worry."

"Something sort of did, in a way. A little bit of extra cash, enough, I hope, to put away so Fin can go to football camp."

"Really?" Simon said, munching on chips covered with Colman's. "What's happened?"

"A lot happened today, and actually we need to discuss my job later. But the shocking bit is our neighbour came to the door and asked could we let her a garden plot."

"You're having me on! Witchy woman paid a call, did she?" Simon said, leaving the table. He didn't mind doing the washing up as the warm water sometimes felt good on his hands. He squirted a bit of apple-scented Fairy Liquid into the sink, and regretted not being here to meet the illustrious woman.

"She offered a hundred pounds, and I told her that was far too dear, that I'd not take half that much. She didn't have all of the necessary tools, you see, so she wanted to cover the cost of using ours, whatever that means. Naturally, I told her that was nonsense and that she was welcome to them. And I said she could use our water, and so on. We settled on seventy-five, and she seemed to think that was a bargain."

"Hmm."

"But that's not the real news." Lorna's voice dropped, and she turned to check that the children were absorbed in watching the television. "I went to old Miss Harrop's place."

"Oh, dear. Visiting with the whole coven, are you?"

"Simon, do grow up. She was collapsed. Lying on her kitchen floor, and for all I knew, dead. I rang for help, and she went to hospital."

"Did she know you were there? What'd they think was wrong with her?"

"She saw me for a flash, but you know she mayn't ever remember. They seemed to think she'd be okay. But you'd never believe what I saw in that house. It was filthy. She's hoarded every bit and bob and all sorts of useless stuff you couldn't imagine, and it's all stacked up in there."

"No, really?"

"Yes. And I've got to do something about it, you know. Avalyn thinks—"

"Avalyn? Would that be the gardening sorceress?"

"Don't call her that. We got on well enough."

"Well enough for you to take her dosh."

"Don't be an ogre, Simon, and listen to my bloody story for heaven's sake. A woman's life is at risk—if she's broken health codes they may push her out of her own home. Avalyn thought I ought to get in touch with Miss Harrop's family before I phone the local council. But we all know they don't come 'round and I can't think how to find them."

Finished, Simon withdrew his hands from the basin and let the water go down the drain. His sister hadn't remembered to dry a single dish as she'd been talking. He took a freshly laundered towel from the drawer and started polishing the drinking glasses.

"That's rather simple," he told her. "I was at school with her nephew, he lived right here in the village till his father got a job in the Far East and the family based themselves in London. Hugo was several years older than me, that's why you don't remember. He's something in finances. No, wait, I know. Business intelligence is his line. Essentially, it's managing credit cards on a corporate level. Dominique and I came across him one afternoon at a pub in Narrow Street."

"Are you saying his name is Hugo Harrop? That'll be an easy enough one to remember."

Simon was becoming fatigued. He moved over to the table, planted his hands, and eased himself down onto a chair. It hardly felt better, but he refused to carry about the special chair that a well-meaning occupational health counsellor kept banging on about. He'd also passed on the benefits offered, but if he didn't get a job soon then perhaps he ought to get on the dole, for the sake of his sister and the children.

"What do you want from Hugo?"

"I should think that's obvious—his aunt needs help. The poor old dear—"

Simon's laughter rang out and interrupted the children. They abandoned their show and came running, wanting to know what their uncle found so funny. Peony jumped onto his knee, and his laughter was louder for a moment, covering up a yelp of pain.

"What's so funny?" Finley said. His interest was waning already, as the next show came up, one of his favourites.

"Nothing you need to know," Lorna said. "Haven't you any homework? You've got geography and maths, I expect."

"I suppose," Finley mumbled, obediently making for the stairs. Simon suddenly felt very proud of his sister, and proud of the great kids she was bringing up. And she'd been doing it all on her own. Till now, anyway, he thought. He'd find a way to help her. He was glad to be part of her family, living under the same roof. Peony leaned back against his chest, and he hugged her small body tightly.

Chapter Six

CLEARING OUT THE workshop, which his father had run as a service and repair garage, was going slowly, but Simon enjoyed seeing the chaos come to order. He'd never closed his own workshop without tools being put away, the floors swept clean, and orders properly placed in a queue on the board and labeled as being done, in progress, or flagged as new. His staff had known keeping the workshop tidy was non-negotiable. Bringing his father's old garage back to an efficient state had actually been rather easy once Simon organised the workbench. It came down to lots of small items going in the dustbin, having a rest and a drink, and then going at it for a few more minutes. Simon wanted the cleared out building to be good for something, but, at the moment, he couldn't reckon what that use would be. Unlike Avalyn Smith, whose cottage happened to have a tiny garden consisting mainly of a dog run and no outbuildings, surrounded by someone else's field, most people in the area had plenty of storage room. On good days, he imagined using the space for building furniture. On bad days, he wondered if he'd ever be able to do much in the way of manual labour again. At least for the moment, he felt as though he was accomplishing something. Although Lorna didn't care much about the workshop, it was on the property, so Simon felt that he was providing her a benefit.

There was one small area left, and he'd be finished cleaning the workshop. He spied a canvas in the back corner, and walked over to it. Dragging off the dusty material, he discovered a vintage Panther motorcycle, laying on its side. Simon wondered how it'd come to his father's garage, but it really wasn't too unbelievable as his dad had been left with an assortment of motors over the years, when people couldn't pay for the work he'd done on them or had some other change in circumstances. Simon supposed that Finley would enjoy helping him restore it, especially since it looked to be in pretty good nick. It was relatively free from rust, and had most of its parts intact. He put the cover back on, and wondered if it was nigh on impossible to get parts for a motorcycle of that age. Or how he could possibly afford them.

Then Simon had an idea.

Avalyn filled Gus's dish with fresh water and smoothed his glistening white fur beneath her palm. He panted lightly, his jaw slack and his ears flopped in relaxed contentment. It had been a wonderful day. She'd had a new patient from the village, Mrs. Venner, who came on the recommendation of Emily Norcross. They'd had a good consultation. Avalyn suspected Mrs. Venner would be better able to manage her diabetes as she followed the changes in diet that Avalyn prescribed. Avalyn found her clinical work most exciting but wished that she could afford to leave the business side of things to someone else. Despite her ability to comprehend complex scientific concepts, she found interfacing with the healthcare system remarkably hard going. As a result, she was tired this evening.

She left Gus circling down for a nap and walked the short distance to Lorna Whiston's property. The late summer weather was still holding, and the air was mild and smelled deliciously of sunshine on grass. Birds sang and wheeled in small groups from one clump of trees to another. Distractedly, Avalyn plucked a wild foxglove from the edge of the ditch and studied its blue-purple petals, her thoughts turning to her new allotment and all of the potential it represented. She'd tuck in spinach as soon as she could, to get a harvest before the frosts of mid October. Randomly, she speculated on how many patients she may come to treat between now and then, and pondered about whether or not the village would seem more like home by the time the spinach came in. As she passed the Whistons grey farmhouse, she considered digging in a few flower bulbs. She was thinking about which flowers to choose, based on what she could cut and bring into her office, as she rounded the corner to look over her plot.

But what she saw brought her up short.

A tall, rather handsome man had just finished cutting away an oblong of grass with a turf cutter. The motor still running, he was doing something to the machine and hadn't yet noticed her. Avalyn was in little doubt that the man was Lorna's brother. She could see their resemblance when he turned his head. The outline of his fine nose was the same as his sister and both her children, his hair the same brown shade as Peony's. Perspiration damped his chambray shirt, and it clung between his shoulder blades. He was lean and rather powerful looking. Avalyn had heard whispers about Lorna's brother, but nothing she could make sense of, other than the fact that he returned to the community under some hardship. He'd been scarce in the village. She wasn't even sure of his name.

The turf had been removed as neatly as a puzzle piece. The aromatic, excess lawn lay in rolls and heaps. He'd cut the perimeter of her garden plot the perfect size, a few feet distant from the shade of a large mulberry by the fencerow so that her veg would thrive in full sun. Either Lorna gave him exact instructions based on their conversation, or this man had green fingers, and knew instinctively how it ought to be done. She dared hope it was the latter.

His task complete, he switched off the machine and stopped moving. She was about to speak, then thought better of it, for he'd taken a step back, and a hand, still encased in a brown leather glove, flew to his hip, pressing. Avalyn recognized the gesture of trying to calm pain, applying pressure on the agitated nerves for a small, desperate measure of comfort. She turned to walk away, affording him privacy to overcome the worst of it.

But as she turned, so did he.

His face quickly melted into a warm, charming smile. "You've caught me out, working your new plot." His deep voice was friendly.

Avalyn smiled in return and came closer, and was enveloped in the smell of freshly dug earth and spicy aftershave. She laughed and something quite pleasant passed between them as she looked into his eyes. "I am very grateful. You've saved me hours of work, figuring out the size of it and turning the lawn as you've done."

"My pleasure, Miss."

She offered her hand. "Avalyn Smith. You're Lorna's brother?"

He removed his glove and joined his hand to hers. "Yes. Simon Whiston, head garden plotter. I don't suppose Lorna showed you where anything is kept?"

"No, she didn't."

"Come 'round here, then. You'll be pleased to see what's waiting for you." He smiled at her again, and Avalyn's cheeks flushed as she frantically tried to remember if people had spoken of him being married. There was something about a woman. What was it?

They walked back in the direction of the house, and Simon led her towards a large, timbered outbuilding that Avalyn imagined was a barn, garage, or workshop of some sort. When they got closer, he strayed to the left, away from the road. There was a creaky wooden gate, and she followed him through. He then stopped and faced her, sending her heart cantering when he smiled. He gestured to the left, indicating that she turn the corner behind the building. She could see that he savoured her suspense.

Behind the outbuilding lay a secret garden. Although long neglected, its old bones were lovely.

"What a surprise," Avalyn said, surveying the beech hedge surrounding the space, and the gravel walks that were taken over in places by weeds. Four paths converged in the centre where a bronze sundial stood in a large circle of bedding. Around the dial were dozens of striking flowers that had overcome two of the wedge shaped borders and engulfed the sundial's pedestal.

"Oh my, what are those?"

"If memory serves, the taller ones are 'Bishop of Llandaff' dahlia, with the scarlet flower and bronze foliage. And the wine colored variety are called 'Dark Desire'."

It had been a long while since something as simple as hearing a man say the name of a flower caused a flutter of sensations. She crossed her arms in front of her chest and walked towards the dial, gaining some distance from Simon Whiston, under the pretence of taking a closer look at the plants.

He casually followed.

"Here, I've got some cutters that I was using in the garage earlier." He reached into a pocket, and gently placed a pair of heavy secateurs into her hand. "Clip whatever you'd like for a bouquet. They keep pretty well."

"Oh, lovely, Simon, thank you." *The first time I've said his name*, she thought, as she selected some blooms and cut them. She ought to feel silly, observing that sort of trivial detail, but she felt too much pleasure to feel ridiculous.

There were tall, leggy hydrangea with some dried bowls of flowers, perfectly preserved on their stems, day lilies of unusual colours, and roses. Simon pointed to the long wall of the garden opposite them. "Those are Golden Shower roses, still blooming like mad, over there by the wall. A few might set off the sort of wine and purple colours in your bouquet."

Avalyn responded, "You're a gardener, aren't you? As well as possessing a good sense of colour?"

"Oh, I don't know, I suppose a bit," Simon said, obviously pleased by her observation. "I know most people lay out a garden to be seen from the house. This one was here so that my Mum could run the office when Dad's garage was up and running, and still be able to nip out to the garden. Lorna and I played here quite a bit, with the Graham children who lived in your cottage, before we were old enough to be off to school. This little plot was her pride and joy, and, I expect, a bit of a stress reliever, too. Later she expanded it quite a bit, and I helped her build it and do the planting. It was something to do, you know, out here where entertainment is scarce."

Avalyn carefully added roses to her bouquet and returned the secateurs.

"There's more I want to show you," he said, leading the way out of another gate on the far side of the garden.

Avalyn trailed behind him on the narrow path hoping he would tell her more about his mother. The abundance of flowers that she'd gathered were fragrant and beautiful, and made her feel as rich as the Queen. Simon paused, and she looked up. There was an enchanting little potting shed, full of tools hanging neatly along the wall, and small terra cotta pots in stacks, as well as plastic trays for starting seeds. A couple of sturdy cold frames stood against the shed, their glass tops perfect for catching the early rays of spring sunshine, keeping seedlings warm, protected, and nourished until they grew mature enough to sow into the earth. Simon turned to her, smiling. "You're free to use anything, only I am afraid it's rather far away from your garden. There's a cart. You'll find the tap on the side of the house, and there's a hose, there, for watering when you need."

"This is wonderful, Simon. Cheers."

"Our pleasure." She didn't know whether he said "our" because he felt shy, or rather because it seemed to him to be more Lorna's property than his.

Chapter Seven

LORNA WHISTON WASN'T very handy with the Internet, so her best mate, Emily, had gotten the telephone number for her. Hugo Harrop's office in London boasted a very smart address, Emily said, which elicited a remark from Lorna about how he ought to be well able to help his poor auntie.

A woman with a greeting that sounded like a recording put through Lorna's call, and a man with a smooth, masculine voice answered.

"Mr. Harrop, this is Lorna Whiston, from Burleigh Cross. You may remember my older brother, Simon, being a few years younger than you, at the village school?"

"Yes, I recall your brother. More importantly, I've recently learnt *your* name."

This was not what Hugo Harrop in London was meant to say, and it threw her. Further, she wasn't expecting him to sound so kind whilst saying something so disagreeable. What was *that* supposed to mean?

"Well, uh…"

"You see, I've been speaking with my great-aunt, and she mentioned you."

"Oh. I wasn't sure she'd remember me, you know, when I found her."

"She did remember you calling for an ambulance. And that's not all she said, of course." There was a soft laugh, and then he said, "I suppose you're wanting to know how she's getting on?"

"No. I mean, yes, of course. How is she, Mr. Harrop?"

"Please, it's Hugo." His voice was patient, not at all the hassled and harried tone she'd expected from a successful man in the City. "She's improved, thank you. I haven't actually seen her, I've been rather tied up here. There's a big contract we're working on."

So, he was harried, but not hassled with the sense of duty to family.

"Oh, yes, of course," Lorna replied, as though contracts, mergers, and million dollar deals were part of her everyday life.

A long pause fell between them. She imagined he was reading email and hadn't noticed.

Lorna took a decision; it was time to get on task. "Mr. Harrop, er, Hugo, you're probably not aware that your aunt is living in a total dustbin. She mustn't be allowed to go home, not with the state everything's in."

"Really?"

"Yes, really. Every health code ever written stands to have been violated in her cottage. It actually *smells*."

Lorna heard another round of soft laughter at the other end of the phone. "I didn't think it was amusing, Hugo, when I saw what… well, what I saw." She could feel the drum of her pulse in her neck. The Harrop family had a way of annoying her beyond reason.

"My apologies. Please, continue with what you were saying, Miss Whiston. It is Miss?"

"What? Yes. Well. I am just ringing to see what you intend to do. Old—your aunt—will probably be released from hospital soon, and it may already be too late. I mean, it may already be that the ambulance blokes have contacted the authorities."

"Right. Thank you for bringing it to my attention."

"So, you didn't know?"

Hugo seemed to be gathering his thoughts. "No, she wasn't likely to tell me, was she? Family hasn't been allowed to set foot in that house for years. It was certainly Providence that you were there to assist her, and I am indebted to you."

"Now what?"

"Pardon?"

"Well, what do you intend doing about it?"

"I am not sure I follow."

"I called to offer my help, Mr. Harrop. I am a cleaner, and if you could arrange for a skip to take away the... *stuff*, and help me to pay a couple of friends—because I can't manage it on my own—then I can sort this out for your aunt."

"Why would you want to do that?"

Lorna wasn't sure. She said, "I am not sure. I suppose I am feeling neighbourly. I care about how an old lady gets on. I suppose I can't reckon *why you don't care*, as she's your aunt!"

"Yes. I'll give it some thought, and I appreciate the call. Goodbye."

He rang off. Lorna sat for some minutes, unable to get her head around the fact that he'd just dismissed her. Abruptly. "What a prat," she whispered. Simon had said that he was a decent sort, so what was she meant to think of his response?

Seething, she rang him up again. The otherworldly receptionist put her right through to Hugo without any show of surprise. Mister Hugo Harrop, sitting in his posh office, didn't care a fig about his dear old auntie. Of course, Miss Harrop was the worst sort of old biddy, but still, Lorna felt indignant on her behalf, on behalf of the aged and abused everywhere, in fact.

"What sort of response was that?"

Hugo's tones were measured and firm. "You are nothing if not aggressive. I didn't believe you'd actually struck my aunt in the street; honestly, I *had* thought she was exaggerating. Nevertheless, this is not a very pressing issue with *me*, although you obviously feel differently, Miss Whiston."

"How can it not be a pressing issue? Why don't you care about the condition of your aunt's home?"

"Because she's not returning home. Now, if you'll excuse me.

Again."

The call was disconnected.

Simon collected the children from Emily's. Finley recounted the day's science lesson, something about surface tension, and why the bathtub gets sludgy. Simon's attention wandered as he tried to give his nephew the impression that he was listening.

It had been a rather discouraging day. He'd finished tidying the workshop, which left his spirits soaring. But then he'd spent the afternoon at the unemployment help centre, which was rather spirit crushing. He had few skills outside of carpentry. And although he'd managed a successful business, applying that acumen elsewhere seemed risky to prospective employers. He despised the routine of driving to Maidstone, checking in at the desk, and carrying himself off to sit in a rather torturously uncomfortable metal chair whose faux leather had flattened considerably under the weight of the masses. Then he was called back to a depressing office and shuffled into another chair, bright orange, no less, and given a hopeless review from a bored employee. At least that part of the process hadn't been quite as horrible. Today, he'd been reviewed by a sweet old lady called Doris. She'd actually applied her meagre energies to helping him. Not that she'd helped.

"They just don't like a manager with dodgy health," said Doris, the kindly lady at the job seeker's centre. Simon wondered how she'd managed to keep a job as she looked well past the usual retirement age.

She'd sighed and told him, "I've got arthritis, too, you know."

Perhaps I could have your job, then? he thought.

He felt guilt for the cheeky thought when Doris then removed her glasses, in a sort of show of despair and sympathy, the thin skin of her wrinkled forehead bunched in concern for him.

"Well, I can hardly blame them," Simon replied, trying to make her feel better about the people who wouldn't give him a chance.

"You're not listening." Finley's voice broke into his thoughts.

"I am sorry, Fin. I've got a lot of my mind."

"You mean that you haven't found a job."

Simon looked at his nephew and couldn't help but smile. "You, boy, are very perceptive."

"I told my teacher. He was at school with you. Mr. Peachey."

"Fin, you didn't."

Simon brought the van to a stop at a junction. His nephew was fiddling with a piece of paper brought home from school. Obviously, the boy was shaken to think he'd upset Simon.

"Well, what'd he say, then? Any ideas?"

"No. He said he'd think about it."

"Cheers, Fin. Leave it to me to get a job, though, okay mate? Don't fret yourself."

"I was only trying to help."

"I know."

Lorna stood up from her chair and went to put the kettle on.

Simon came in. "Perfect timing," he said with an annoying sort of cheerfulness.

"Hugo Harrop has no intention of doing anything to help his aunt, can you believe it?"

"You've called him, then? What did he say?"

"Quite simply that he wasn't concerned about it, that she wasn't coming back to live in her house, anyway. Oh dear!" Lorna put the milk down and turned to her brother, who was washing his hands. "You don't think she's died?"

"Possibly, but it seems he would have said. Or, that it'd be known around the village, and you've only just been to Goodchild's this morning. Why's there no cola?"

"Because I don't want you drinking it in front of Finley. Stop making faces—I saw Jamie Oliver on TV and I've developed an unholy fear of excess sugar. Perhaps no one from the village has known how to get in touch with Miss Harrop? What if he's putting her in some dreadful care home?"

"I doubt he would do that, as expensive as it all is, if she could live on her own. And Chef Oliver can sod off. I rather enjoy excesses of sugar."

"Suppose they won't let her return to the house? Those

ambulance workers could have reported her."

Simon beamed like a jester.

"Don't you mock me, Simon. She's an abandoned old lady, and I am trying to help, no matter what's passed between us. It's what neighbours are meant to do."

"Hmm. Some people ask their neighbour to come for dinner. More to the point, a tall, blonde, gorgeous neighbour, one very grateful for help with her garden."

"Avalyn? Really?"

"Yes, really. She's asked me for next week. Meantime, she must to go to London for a couple of days."

Lorna made tea. "I can see it on your face. You really do fancy her?"

"The proverbial torch lit immediately."

"How fitting," Lorna said, giggling. "You've been seen toppling a bit, you know, a moment of being unsteady on your feet. So, the pair of you'll be known as the sloppy drunk and the village witch, while I go about smacking down the elderly—we're quite a name in these parts!"

Simon chuckled with her.

They sat down to tea. He suddenly asked, "When were you last involved with anyone?"

"Oh, not since before Peony was born."

"Why Lorna? You're quite pretty, and, when you want to be, incredibly sweet."

"I was in love with Rowan, you know. Thought he'd stay. But as soon as I told him we'd started a baby, off he went. I never told you, but I couldn't cope for a while. All that money you sent, when things were going so well with your business? Fin and I lived on it for some while. I was able to get out of bed, do the essentials, but I wasn't working, or even going into the village. I'd taken leave, and told my supervisor it was pregnancy related. Emily did the shopping, and I'd reimburse her. It was a dark time."

Simon reached out and took her hand.

"I am glad to have helped, even though I hadn't a clue. And I have to say, although I don't know what my future holds, I want us to be close. Maybe Mum might even come back from Australia, when Aunt Ida doesn't need her help with Uncle Trevor any longer."

Again, Lorna was overcome by giggles. "If she knew what people were saying about us, she wouldn't show her face!"

As Lorna readied herself for bed, her mobile rang.

"Hello?"

"You, feisty girl, whatever your name is. He's put me in care, and they won't let me leave. You'll come and collect me, won't you? You owe me—"

"Miss Harrop? Is that you?"

"I am going home, girl. You'll—"

Lorna could hear another voice in the background. Soothing, "Miss Harrop, dear, you know you're not allowed to make calls at this hour." The line went dead.

Chapter Eight

LORNA AND EMILY returned to the Whistons' farmhouse with their children. Finley had been ecstatic to see a mummy featured at the museum in Maidstone. Peony didn't care much for a person covered in bandages, but she rather liked creating shapes with scissors and coloured papers, then pasting them to form a collage, in the children's activities room. The women had treated the children to lunch in a café before returning home to relax over a cup of tea.

Emily sat rocking her baby, Bethany, who had drifted off to sleep, while Lorna nestled in the corner of her comfy gold sofa. Finley and Peony had brought home a plastic tote of treasures from the museum, and now had papers, artwork, and brochures scattered about the rug, as a means of review. Peony wanted to get her scissors and cut up the brochures to make more Matisse inspired creations, and Finley was reading aloud from a brochure about upcoming exhibitions.

A knock came at the door. Lorna and Emily exchanged inquiring glances. "Hmm…" Lorna said, walking through the sitting room and towards the front door beyond the kitchen. She opened it to a man of medium height, bearing the largest bouquet of flowers that Lorna had ever seen sans casket.

"My word, did someone die?"

The man grinned as though he were very charmed indeed, but said nothing as he handed them to her.

"For me? Oh, dear. And I suppose you'll be wanting a tip for your trouble? Let me get my purse."

"No...no, that won't be necessary."

She paused and gave the man a once over. Indeed, she had made a mistake. He was wearing a suit. A well-tailored, looks-a-million-pounds sort of suit. Not the sort of attire for delivering out of a van. Emily, cradling a sleeping Bethany, had materialized beside her.

The man in the suit held out his hand. "Lorna Whiston? I am Hugo Harrop."

"Oh! My goodness, are you really?" Lorna said, laughing, her hand flying to her throat in embarrassment. "This is my friend, Emily Norcross, and her daughter, Bethany." Lorna composed herself and shook his hand. Hugo smiled obligingly, the way one does when introduced to an infant. "Won't you come in, Mr. Harrop?"

"I shouldn't like to intrude."

Lorna and Emily smiled at him, then at one another.

"Its no trouble, we see each other often, and we've been out all day with the children. Please. Come in, have a cup of tea."

Unsure of where else to put the costly garden she held in her arms, Lorna turned on the taps and settled the bouquet into the deep farmhouse sink. She smiled, thinking perhaps she could locate a small *bucket* for them later. Emily was clearing off, taking the children outside to play. Dear Em.

She turned and looked at the dishy man seated incongruously at her table, and felt both nervous and excited at once.

"I should explain," Hugo Harrop began. Lorna lingered by the kettle, feeling rather self-conscious. She wished her kitchen were tidier, but they'd wanted something with their tea. Emily had brought a delicious apple sponge, the crumbs of which were scattered around Hugo's folded, executive looking hands. She turned her back to make the tea, and he paused, waiting for her full attention.

Feeling as clumsy as a waitress-in-training, she carefully placed their cups and saucers on the table, and sat opposite him, gazing at nothing in particular to avoid his eyes. Which were green, she'd happened to notice. One does, sometimes.

"Obviously, the flowers were your first clue," began Hugo. "I am here to apologise. I didn't mean to act so appallingly when you rang the other day. You caught me at rather a bad time, I'm afraid. We're in the middle of a merger, and although it's gone rather well, the horrid process runs on for days. Loads of pressure. Please forgive me."

"I'd rather thought I was the one who ought to apologise to you, but I'd already rang you up twice as it was!"

They shared a laugh, and the tension eased. Lorna felt quite like herself, now, and stole a long look into his eyes. Green with flecks of gold. Intense. Very nice, indeed.

"I've another reason for coming," Hugo said. "I've given some thought to what you said on the phone. If your offer stands, I'd very much like to have you, and a staff, clear out the house. You'd be well-paid, naturally, and have whatever you need for the project."

"I'd be happy to help. But, you said that your aunt isn't returning? What does that mean, exactly?"

"The doctors felt some tests were necessary. They've determined she isn't well enough to stay on her own. I'd noticed that she was a bit confused when I spoke to her a few months ago, but apparently she's worse off than I imagined. We've found a care home for her."

Lorna considered this. It was difficult to imagine old Miss Harrop being looked after. "Was she awfully upset?"

"Surprisingly, no. She seemed relieved, and said something about feeling that she wasn't up to scratch. Complained of feeling exhausted."

"That's not what she told me," Lorna said, crossing her arms and watching her visitor very carefully. "She phoned me and told me she was being held against her will, and some care giver disconnected us."

Hugo carried on. "Well, as I said, she's had some dotty moments. Her mood seems to change constantly, but the doctors say that's to be expected." Seeming to feel as though he'd dealt her enough of an explanation, Hugo Harrop skillfully changed tact. It wasn't difficult to imagine him having a cool head in challenging business situations. "You'd mentioned her having a cat? She didn't even ask about it, as though she'd forgotten him."

"I set out a bit of food for him, but he'll need a new home."

"Those darling children of yours, wouldn't they want to keep him?" Hugo said with a smile.

Charming smile or no, Lorna quickly replied, "That, dear sir, is the last thing I need." He chuckled and she thought again that he really was rather handsome. And she'd always loathed that old woman, so why be bothered over her being sent to a home?

"Suppose he came with kitty support—a few pounds for a fresh box, food, and so on?"

"Now you're making me feel quite guilty," Lorna said. She'd nearly forgotten how to flirt, or so she thought, but realised that she was looking at Hugo through her eyelashes.

"I've got a proposition for you that might induce more guilt."

"Hugo! What *are* you talking about?" Terribly clumsy. But she was having fun, and he didn't seem to notice.

"Perhaps your friend could be persuaded to mind the children a little longer. I'd be honoured if you'd come out to dinner with me, Lorna."

Her heart sped.

They fixed things with Emily, Lorna changed, and minutes later they were driving towards Burleigh Cross in Hugo's car. Lorna was surprised that Hugo had wanted to come to the village pub. The George & Dragon was, in fact, owned by a man called George Wilson, Jr, who had it from his father, George Wilson the second; who had had the pub from his father, George Wilson. The two-story pub was very old, with a distinguished crisscrossed brick design beneath a brownish-red tiled roof, and, on the ground floor, rows of black timber stripes queued across whitewashed plaster. The baskets of flowers hanging on either side of the doorway welcomed September with profuse red, white, and purple blooms. Inside the pub, there were numerous corners in which to hide away, low beams clung to the snug ceilings, and, in the winter, several old fireplaces warmed the cosy rooms. Lorna followed Hugo across the thick carpets that ran up to oak-paneled walls. He walked back a few paces and shook hands with several men seated at the bar who'd recognised him and called out greetings. They found a table by the window, which gave a lovely view onto the green.

Each George who'd been the pub's proprietor had attended a proper chef's school of their day, and each took great satisfaction in using fresh local ingredients. However, by some continued preference through the generations, each George had refused to change their entrees and upset the regular punters. As a result, neither Hugo nor Lorna consulted the menu, which never changed beyond seasonal vegetables and the soup of the day, and gave their orders.

Meeting Hugo had been such a surprise that only now did it dawn on Lorna that dining with Miss Harrop's nephew would surely be a topic of conversation throughout the village.

"It occurs to me that this may help my reputation a bit. Or perhaps damage yours."

"What do you mean?"

"Hugo, you're just being sweet. After the way I treated your aunt? You might as well know there are a few people around here that consider me the village tart."

"Are you?"

"Hugo!" But she smiled back at him.

"I am not totally out of the loop with life in the village, Miss Whiston. My mates tell a different tale about you."

"What's that?" Lorna swilled a gulp of water. The pub seemed unusually quiet, and she fought the urge to escape his gaze and scan the room. Her emotions were running the gambit of being delighted at being out with a handsome, successful man, to feeling inferior and worrying things might not be as they seem. "Tell me your worst."

"I am told that Rowan O'Riordan behaved like a swine. He's in London now, working at the docks, and he's earned a reputation as a real bounder."

Lorna tested him. "It could have been my fault. No one outside of our relationship really knows. Perhaps he was a decent sort, until he met me and I ruined him for life."

"No sweetie, I don't think so. A chap who's happy as a lark one day, living in, committed, and then he's gone? Suspicious, to say the least. Especially when it becomes obvious there was baby news. That's how the lads say it was, a very sudden change of plans for O'Riordan. And you seeming to all the world a woman very much in love, a woman incapable of cheating. A nice girl who got blindsided."

Lorna felt tears begin to prick in her eyes.

Hugo leaned in. "Why does it bother you that people know *he* behaved badly? Even more, why are you trying to suggest you're also to blame?"

"Well, I could hardly be blindsided—I'd had Finley already, and had been through his father walking out. I suppose I must confess, his leaving was something of a shock," Lorna said, dabbing a stray tear with her fingertip. "I didn't realise I'd signed on for psychoanalysis over dinner," she joked, but Hugo waited. She was astonished by his interest. She didn't know him, but found herself confiding in him, in the way that it's sometimes easier to speak about important things with a stranger.

"I felt so used, so foolish. The thing I've never been able to get my head around is that he'd accepted my son from a previous relationship, so why leave when we found out I was having *his* baby?"

Hugo Harrop covered Lorna's hand in his. "I think it says a lot about him. Perhaps, in his thinking, the relationship had run its course and having a baby didn't give him pause because he's simply that selfish." Hugo smiled, but at his lap instead of at his date. His face winced in an expression of regret. "It's time for me to apologise, again. I've only just met you less than an hour ago, and I am raking through a painful time in your life. I simply wanted to say that people don't think so badly of you as you'd imagine, Lorna. And I don't mind being seen with you here, or I shouldn't have brought you."

She sniffed, and then giggled. "Alright. Just one question, though, Mr. Harrop. Why were you talking with your mates about me?"

"There you've found me out. The truth is, if you weren't a hard-working, responsible sort of person, I wouldn't have bothered to drive from London and discuss my aunt's house with you. And I freely admit, I was asking around, vetting you for the job of clearing out the house. As it happens, Sam Stockton said he thought you'd make a good job of it, and that you're a delightful girl as well. I may have also remembered that Simon's younger sister was quite pretty."

"Sam Stockton! I'd quite forgotten about him. How is he?"

"Very well. We're quite a small fraternity, you know. Those half-dozen of us who've left the village. Your brother included."

The server brought their meals.

"Well, I am not sure it counts if one comes back," Lorna said, slicing into a tender piece of beef. "Simon has, you know. He's living with us at the farmhouse."

They talked for a while about her brother, and other people they knew.

Hugo asked questions about his aunt's home and what Lorna thought should be done with it. "I went over and had a bit of a look around, but honestly, I didn't want to carry away any muck on my suit. It was quite a sight. You didn't exaggerate."

"I am not at all certain how big the job will be until we get in there," Lorna said. "Honestly, I am also not entirely sure that myself, and any cleaners that I can bring on to help, are quite up to the task. It's hard to say what's lurking in that house. Perhaps there are specialist firms for properties like this?"

Hugo took a sip of beer. He'd tucked into the roast duck with butter beans, rocket salad and crusty bread on his plate with enthusiasm. Forking beans, he laughed and said, "Ah, so the lovely Lorna's got a good business head, eh?"

Lorna was pleased at his compliment.

"You're quite right. My secretary, Margaret, did some checking for me this afternoon. She found a company that would extend their reach a bit and come to Burleigh Cross. For a price, naturally. They do clearance, valuation, and deal with the bulk of the rubbish disposal. That'll include taking away broken TVs or her primeval microwave, or whatever else needs dealing with. Margaret was told over seventy-five percent of what comes out of most properties can be either donated to a local charity, refurbished and used, or recycled, so don't fear for the local landfill."

"Yes, that would've kept me up nights," Lorna joked. She realised then she'd quite forgotten to make a start on her meal, and picked up her knife and fork.

"They're coming on the fourth."

"No grass growing under your feet."

"It's the ever-efficient Margaret that gets the credit for sorting it out. Which brings us on to you. I still need help in the form of a cleaner and a sort of consultant. They told Margaret a basic, deep clean would be in order after they're through, so that seems suited to your offer to help. The firm that handles removal also requires someone they can consult for particular decisions, say, supposing the carpet could be salvaged then they'd want to know, would we rather it be cleaned and salvaged, or do we prefer it to be removed, that sort of thing. If you wouldn't mind to be that person, I'd be grateful."

Lorna nodded her consent, honoured by his trust in her.

With a sly grin, Hugo added, "Obviously you have my number. However, I'll give you my card, and expect an invoice from you when you've finished. Post it, or email it, in care of Margaret. She'll be phoning with a few more details this week."

They chatted for an hour more and Hugo drove her home. Lorna could scarcely wait to tell Emily everything.

Meantime, her emotions ran hot and cold. She would try her best to sort out what it was that bothered her about Hugo Harrop. Certainly one thing was clear. Her unsettled feelings begged the question: how she could be certain that Miss Harrop truly belonged in a care home?

Chapter Nine

"GOOD JOB, FIN. You're a natural mechanic, like your grandfather."

"Really?"

"Definitely." Simon lowered to his haunches and finished tightening the screws that Finley had started for him. He didn't know the story behind the 1955 Panther 100 he'd found under the tarp, but someone had done an extensive rebuild of most of the pricey parts. Had it been his father? He was able to source some small parts from his dad's inventory. But they were missing a tank, and those didn't come cheap. He hoped his idea of selling some of items in the garage as scrap metal would help finance the part, as well as help in the house.

Finley was rather taken with the papers that Simon had found in his father's old desk. Someone called Chad Thaxter had signed the Panther over to his father several years before Oakley Whiston died.

Finley held the papers in his hands. "I don't write like grandpa, though."

"Well, his writing could've changed, too. I no longer write the same as I did at your age."

"But you've got trouble with your fingers."

"Even so, my writing changed. You know how you're always using your thumbs, playing games? D'you know what'll happen?"

"No. What?"

"You'll have a really horrid signature on your football contract."

Finley's face brightened into a grin, and he stashed the title of the motorcycle back into his uncle's shirt pocket.

"When can we ride?"

"When we've got these two parts on, and then come by a fuel tank somewhere."

"Never, then."

"No, Fin, don't say never. Have faith, boy. It's early days for this cat's restoration, right?"

Finley laughed. "Oh, I almost forgot. I've got something for you."

Simon finished securing the mud flap of the old bike, and laid aside a piece of wood that had protected the tyres from accidental puncture. He tossed the old wrench into his father's toolbox, drew in a breath, and laid a hand on Fin's shoulder as he straightened his legs. It didn't come easy. Once he was on his feet, he shifted his weight from one foot to the other, trying to calm the pain in his knees, ankles, and hips. Finley was holding a piece of paper that he'd produced from the pocket of his jeans.

"What's this, then?"

"Don't be cross, Uncle Simon. I haven't said anything more. Mr. Peachey's kept his promise and gave me this. He thought it was something you could do."

Simon read over the paper, printed from the Internet. It described a part-time job, driving people about in a van owned by the county. People who are unable to drive for some reason, Simon gathered, without access to public transport, needing a lift to and from "essential services." Quite a step down from operating his furniture company, bringing in several millions annually. More to the point, he would be grateful to perform a service job like this. He was as lacking in independence as the people he'd be driving. He needed to put on the right face for his nephew. Aaron Peachey had written the name of a reference person across the top of the paper.

"This is quite thoughtful of Mr. Peachey, and you too, Finley. I'll look into it."

His nephew's relief was evident. What a good lad.

"Let's go see what's for tea, shall we?"

They crossed the drive, walked across the lawn, and entered the back door of the farmhouse, which seemed to be in chaos. Peony was crying, and Lorna was yelling something about how "you'd simply quit trying". Simon jaw tensed as he pushed Finley aside and went striding towards the kitchen. If Rowan O'Riordan or someone else were here giving his sister grief, then he would be made to leave, sharpish.

Finley followed his uncle as far as the end of the passage, where he picked up Peony and looked about for Gemma Giraffe.

Surprisingly, Simon found his own sister alone. Lorna was bent over the ancient white washing machine, hand on either side of it's yawning mouth, looking down at the agitator within. "It's given up."

Simon stepped closer and began his own exploration. "How do you know?"

Lorna straightened. "I've phoned. I've double-checked online. The damn thing's finished, and we need several hundred pound for the cheapest one I could find."

"Oh."

"How could it do this, Simon?"

"It was Granny's. So, it's more than twice your age, for a start."

"There's more."

He closed the lid of the machine, and crossed his arms over his chest.

She took in a deep breath and rubbed her forehead. "I didn't like to tell you. They reduced my hours at the castle. Iona said something about the economy, and shifts changing within the castle, and so those housekeepers took some of our hours at the guest cottages. It's to do with seniority. Believe it or not, some of those birds have been scrubbing away up there for over twenty years. What're we going to do?"

"It's going to be okay, Sis, I promise. Thanks to Finley, I've got a lead on a new job. I've got that bloke coming to collect the old cars and equipment from the workshop. It won't bring much, but certainly enough to buy a new clothes washer, alright? The hours lost at the castle will leave you with more time to clear out the cottage, after Harrop's hired firm has come through."

"I suppose that's true."

He persisted, smiling. "It's not the end of the world, love, just the washing machine. Everything's going to be right as rain. Okay?"

"Alright. But I hope you can get the water out of it. It's full you know."

"No problem. Go be a mum, will you?"

Lorna blessed him with an exhausted smile and turned away.

Chapter Ten

THE DAYS THAT Avalyn Smith spent in London had been fruitful. Her last patient seen and charted, Avalyn unplugged her laptop, extinguished the lights in the borrowed consultation room, and headed for the car park opposite her friend's clinic. The income she'd earned over the past three days was generous, and her mood was light. She stowed the computer in the boot of her car, and decided to treat herself to a meal at her favourite café about a half-mile distant, and then browse around the bookshop on her return.

The early autumn evening was mild. Soon, the days would grow shorter, but for the next several weeks they could count on the night shadows waiting to gather in until at least eight. Even though the traffic light was in her favour, one had to be cautious in crossing the busy London streets during rush hour, where too many impatient drivers were apt to bend the law and pass through after the light had changed. She gratefully reached the opposite pavement, and walked the short distance to the ornate, black, iron gates leading into the park. Avalyn strolled through the park admiring the heavy flush of late roses, their perfume casting notes of myrrh, tangy sweetness, and citrus on the breeze. The sky was cerulean blue, the saturated hue of September that burst in a contrast of colours against yellow leaves.

Birdsong mingled with the muffled sounds of London traffic and little boys called out to each other as they played a game on the lush thick grass. Avalyn thought of Simon Whiston, and felt excited that he'd agreed to come to dinner. She wondered if he felt embarrassed about his situation and, like her, perhaps a bit rusty at romance.

Eager to invite him into her world, she'd gathered her nerve and it all came out in a rush. "Please tell me you'll come to dinner Thursday next," she'd said. "I'll cook us something, and you can tell me more about your mum's garden."

He'd stopped and looked at her. Avalyn had frozen, scanning his face for hints, but his gaze was even and gave away nothing. She'd been so lonely that she hadn't minded the risk when she'd opened her mouth, but in a moment she'd begun to regret saying anything. Had she been too assertive? Or simply surprised him?

Following a pause, Simon had said quietly, "Certainly. What time?"

As she reflected on his response, a big smirk enveloped her face, which certainly had nothing to do with the friendly greetings from the pleasant family who'd just passed by her on the wide path.

She arrived at the café situated in the park. As she collected a sandwich and a bottle of mineral water, she spied a small table outside on the terrace. The sunshine warmed her hair and shoulders as she gazed at the lake and had her tea. The bucolic view, the murmur of other relaxed diners, and the quacking of the mallards on the lake was bliss. She had missed the city, and coming here to the park, but not with a deep homesickness. Perhaps for the first time, Burleigh Cross seemed more like home than London. It was a good feeling; she was glad she'd had the courage to make a change. Although her very new and fragile friendships with the brother and sister across the road played a part, she knew that her contentment was largely drawn from being in the right place. She suddenly decided to give the bookshop a miss. She would leave on the next train, drive to the village, and collect her dog from the kennel. Inwardly, she felt a little fizz of anticipation. She was going home.

The evening of his date with Avalyn finally arrived, and Simon felt it had been a long three days waiting for its coming. It was the first time, in the weeks since he returned to Burleigh Cross, that he noticed a bite of cold. Simon shrugged deeper into his tweed jacket. The early autumn wind held a sprinkling of rain that misted his face. Less than a minute of quitting the farmhouse, he knocked on Avalyn's door.

It opened. She was wearing a lavender jersey with jeans, her hair loose, silky, and falling over one shoulder. "Hello, Simon."

He handed her a bottle of wine and stepped in. The cottage looked much the same: bookshelf heaving with old volumes, walls the colour of raw cotton, and the worn chintz furniture left exactly where it'd always been. There was a new group of cream coloured candles in the fireplace, but it probably wouldn't be long before Avalyn would move them, and stave the autumn chill with a cosy fire. He wondered if she had any wood and made a mental note to deliver some logs from the deep, canvas-covered stack at their farm. Or, rather his sister's farm. His sister had been living there, working there, and raising her children there for years. Any seasoned firewood on the place would be hers, and he would ask her first.

He chided himself. This wasn't the time to feel emasculated by his circumstances, as he was incredibly lucky to be invited by a beautiful woman for a home cooked meal. Pushing himself into the present, he remarked that the cottage seemed more or less the same as when the Grahams were living there.

"I'd wanted to rent a furnished place, so I was happy that all their things were left. Even better, the cottage is really so lovely and to my taste. I like old things, and I didn't have much of my own in London. My flat there was small. Gus's kit filled up the storage in the back garden. He's like having a child, that dog."

"Ah, yes. The ghost dog."

"Ghost dog?"

Simon had opened the wine and began to pour. "Mmm. The night I arrived, you and that gleaming white dog went running across the lane in front of my van. You looked like some sort of apparition."

Avalyn dropped her hands in a sign of helplessness and apology. "Oh, I am sorry, Simon. What's really worrying is that I don't even remember doing it. Nearly being run over has become secondary to my frustration over his roaming about the countryside."

Their dinner had been timed to his arrival, and Avalyn plated the food and brought it to the dark-stained walnut table. Simon ran a finger along the beveled edging of the fine old antique, appreciating its solid craftsmanship. He seemed to remember that the Grahams had had the table from some relations in Scotland, and it had been in this cottage some fifty or more years now. They fanned linen dinner napkins across their laps.

"I hope you don't mind the flavour of ginger?"

"Not at all. I rather like the spiciness of it," Simon said, taking a bite of the salmon that was nestled alongside roasted vegetables dressed in herbs, garlic, and olive oil. Bread plates held crusty bread, and there was farm fresh butter on the table.

"Delicious." Simon tucked into his meal with gusto. Lorna was kind to feed him, but he'd missed food that hadn't come from a tin or a packet retrieved from the deep freeze.

"I am glad it suits."

They talked of Avalyn's practice in the village. She explained her passion for nutrition. "I took several biology courses on various topics. One of them was the nutrition course, and the professor was a thought-provoking instructor. His lectures sparked my interest in the field. I remember he introduced the course by quoting Hippocrates: 'Our food should be our medicine, and our medicine should be our food.' The more I learned, the more I came to agree with that statement."

No one in Simon's family had been to university. Avalyn's open, down to earth attitude made it impossible to be intimidated by her advanced education. He asked her questions. She tactfully avoided bringing forward any scientific studies that may apply to his condition.

As they finished the meal, Simon spoke about his own work in furniture, and his lack of work. "So there you have my life to date. I don't have a bean. Do you want to chuck me out now, or will there be pudding?"

"Something'll turn up," she assured him. He felt infused with hope. Avalyn seemed to have a quiet sort of knowing about things, and it was easy to believe her. He told her about the job description that Finley's teacher had found, for driving people where they needed to go. Not so long ago he wouldn't have considered that type of job, or, if he had, sharing it with an attractive woman certainly wouldn't have come into it.

"You're divorced, is that right?" she asked.

"Well, yes, as it happens, I am." A bitter laugh escaped him. He was surprised for a moment by his own reaction. "I am sorry, I've told one or two close friends that my wife divorced me, but for some reason your question surprised me. It shouldn't have done. I suppose I've sort of kept to myself over these last few years. I don't speak to many people, so perhaps I am out of practice."

He told Avalyn how the last two years had taken him from being happily married to a woman with whom he was in love and in awe, and living in their expansive house on Fulham Palace Road. He related his dismay of being suddenly divorced, living in a soulless, rented flat, and how his health quickly deteriorated. Instead of the creativity and challenge of directing his own prosperous company, he was now a burden to his sister, sleeping in a spare box room with a storabed—in the house to which he would've been hard pressed to call "home."

"It's amazing though, how quickly people adjust. How I have. Certainly, there are still those moments when I think about the past, but really I am all right, you know? A bit of a downer to have 'round to dinner, perhaps, but basically a happy guy." He spoke affectionately about Finley and Peony, and what a great mum his sister was to them. He told her several of the amusing things the children had said recently. Avalyn laughed with him, and it seemed the cobwebs and darkness of the past several years were being swept away in the candlelight dancing between them.

She poured more wine. They took their glasses and moved away from the table to her small sitting room, where they sat quietly for a few minutes.

"Penny for your thoughts, Simon."

"Life is grand. And you're one of the reasons why."

Chapter Eleven

THE FIRM THAT Hugo hired in had done a brilliant job of deciding what ought to stay in his aunt's home, what ought to be binned, and what could be sold. They had even taken away several non-working cookers, which had been occupying a small spare bedroom. The door had had to be removed to get into the room, with the cookers wedged tightly together inside. It was a mystery how that had happened, and how Miss Harrop kept the mountain of rubbish within her home a secret for so many years. The firm left behind various small items, but they had taken away tons of rubbish, giving Lorna a reasonable place to begin sorting through smaller items followed by intense cleaning.

Lorna delighted in working her magic at old Miss Harrop's home. It was similar to the deep cleaning she enjoyed in the spring, those days when sunshine warmed the earth and windows could be thrown open. She placed ear buds in her ears, turned on her favourite pop music, and began the hard slog necessary to bring Miss Harrop's house back to a liveable state. Lorna took advantage of the warm weather to wash windows, which also served to start airing out the house. She banished dust from the tops of doorframes and neglected shelves, laundered heavy winter duvet covers that somehow had never been removed from their original packaging, and hung them outside on the drying green. Later, when she collected them, the linens were scented with the fragrance of baked sunshine. She cleared the fitted cabinets of items deemed worthy of staying on by the property crew. Lorna's days were spent wiping, scrubbing and washing away mildew and dirt from the ceiling, which left her arms and neck aching. She removed stains from the ceramic work surfaces with warm water and vinegar. She coaxed away rust in the stainless steel sink with cream of tartar and lemon juice. The cooker was old, but didn't require repairs, just a thorough sanitising and the sparkle brought back.

Miss Harrop's home was proving to be a satisfying project. Without Lorna's efforts, the house would go on being uninhabitable, and impossible for Hugo to put on the market. That her efforts would impress Hugo Harrop served as a bonus. She'd considered asking some of the women at the castle to help her, but decided to give herself several weeks to see how far she could take the cleaning on her own, and was glad to have a replacement for the hours lost at her usual job cleaning holiday cottages at the castle.

The mess in the house seemed, at times, endless, particularly in the kitchen. Mixing bicarbonate of soda with some lemon scented washing up liquid, Lorna stirred the mixture into a paste. Miss Harrop's cooker had years of glop stuck on, so the thick paste would need a little help. After massaging the paste across the surface, the greasy residue was already beginning to soften. Lorna took a hob scraper and ran it top to bottom in even lines. As she did so, the burnt on mess came away, leaving the cooker clear and clean and looking rather new. She found the results immensely gratifying.

The kitchen table was actually rather nice, and had been protected by the mounds of paper stacked upon it. She cleaned the table and its four chairs, and then polished the old wood with a preparation from her brother until the wood gleamed. Finally, after a vigorous sweeping with a broom, it was time to steam mop the floor.

As she planned to brave the lavatory off the kitchen on her next visit, she made a few preparations. She poured cola into the toilet with the intention of letting it sit in the bowl until she returned. She knew from previous experience, when she'd once cleaned the flat of a nasty bachelor who hadn't done anything to his bathroom in ten years, that cola would remove limescale and build-up. Diluted tea and wiping with a lint-free cloth would restore a spotless shine to the mirrors. Her head was full of these cleaning tasks when she sank into the seat of her car, and slowly reversed out into the lane.

Lorna never saw the speeding vehicle cresting the hill.

Finley came home from school to an empty house. He'd been to practice after school, and expected his mum and sister to be home. The house looked the same, but it felt strange, and walking around made too much noise. He called out, dashed upstairs and then back down, looked out the windows to make certain that Peony wasn't playing on the back lawn, and his mother sitting at the picnic table. Neither were, and he felt a bit of panic. His mum was very regular in her habits and only once, a couple of years ago, had she been detained coming home from her job in Maidstone. But she wasn't working there today.

He searched the kitchen cupboards, looking for a note left by his Mum. She'd probably had to go to the village shop, or maybe she was late collecting his sister from Auntie Emily. There wasn't a note. Unwilling to give up because he didn't have a better idea, he dropped to his knees to search under the kitchen table, and the old phone on the kitchen wall rang.

"Hello? Mum?"

"Hullo there son, would that be Finley Whiston?" said a man, in a sing-song sort of voice.

"Yes."

"I am a first-aider, and we've got your mother here. You're not to worry, but we've taken her to hospital, alright? In Maidstone. In accident and emergency, she is. Are you still there, boy?"

Quite surprised at the news, Finley's heart pound with fear and his eyes immediately teared. He hated that he was crying like a big baby, but the kindly voice on the other end of the line seemed caring.

"Oh. She's okay, though?" Finley sniffed.

"The doctor is lookin' her over now, he is. I don't suppose you've got a granny or someone who'd look after you at home?"

Finley couldn't remember where Uncle Simon was, but he answered yes anyway.

"Okay, lad, well that's good. You go and tell your Granny to call A and E to find out more in a wee bit. Understand, do you?"

"Yes."

Finley stood in the kitchen, feeling totally gutted. Nothing had ever happened to his mum, at least since her last boyfriend left. The boyfriend treated her badly, but she promised she'd never let that happen again, and it hadn't. Somehow, Finley hadn't considered the possibility of anything else ever happening to her.

Tears still burned his eyes, so he knew that he hadn't imagined the call, but as he wiped them away, he wasn't quite as fearful. In mere seconds, he took stock of his life. No matter what happened to his mum, he would be there to help. And he knew his Uncle Simon considered them family. He wouldn't leave them on their own. It was sort of like he and Peony had a dad now. It's what he'd always wanted.

Uncle Simon had made him feel safe, just by being in the house. Finley hadn't really thought about it much. Having Uncle Simon living with them had made all the difference.

His granny was on the other side of the world. Had the man really meant for Finley to try to reach her? Mum said talking to her once a month was expensive. Granny didn't text, and she didn't use computers, so nothing else was any good. Finley looked out the kitchen window. It was still sort of summery, but clear and chilly, too. He turned and looked around the empty kitchen. It looked pretty. Even though there was nothing posh in their house, it looked like a king's ransom in the golden light.

Suddenly it occurred to Finley that he needed to get to Maidstone. To the hospital. He could call Auntie Emily, but she would want him to wait. They always had to wait while she did something with her baby. Babies took forever to pack for the car. And if she came, they'd have to deal with Peony. This situation was for older people, like himself.

Maybe the witch across the lane?

Finley knew that his uncle had been to dinner at her house. She must be okay, and not really a witch. A bit strange, perhaps, but she looked nice enough and she had a car. He knew that she was usually home by this hour, from her office in the village.

He left a note for Uncle Simon, and still wasn't able to remember where he'd got to. He grabbed a biscuit from the tin, and made his way out the door at a run. He knocked on the door of the witch's cottage, while trying to remember her name.

The door opened, and Finley fell silent.

"Hello, Finley. Come in," she said. Finley stepped in her house. It smelled of something good cooking, and her big dog came to greet him, his tail thumping against the woman's leg, and her not minding. Finley decided this had been a good idea. He took the biscuit from his pocket and discreetly fed it to the dog.

"His name is Gus," the lady said. Finley stroked the dog's shiny white fur, and marvelled at the size of his face.

"His head must be as big as a bear," Finley said.

The lady laughed. "Yes, I am sure you're right."

Then she said, "I've baked chocolate chip cookies. Would you like some, with a glass of milk?"

"Yes, please, Miss."

As she poured, the urgency of his mission came back to him. "My mum is in hospital, and I need to get there. Do you suppose you could take me to Maidstone?"

The lady handed him the glass. "Oh my heavens, Finley. Well, of course! I'll help in any way I can." Finley explained about the phone call. The lady listened calmly. He remembered that she was some sort of nurse or doctor or something, which was good. When he finished telling all that he knew, he was thirsty and drank the milk in one go.

The lady called the hospital and asked for information. She got Auntie Emily's number from Finley and rang her, telling her to please look after Peony a bit longer. She texted someone. Then she put Gus in his run, and she and Finley got into her car.

Avalyn's prediction had come true. Thanks to a tip from Finley's teacher, Peachy, Simon was employed. He didn't mind the new job. Twice a week he spent the day driving people in a minibus to wherever they needed to go, within a certain distance. The people varied: there was a twenty-something bloke with autism that Simon drove to twice-a-week college courses, a middle-aged man going to drugs counselling, and a young single mum with a child needing appointments with an allergy specialist. Once, he'd even taken a famous nun to the airport.

It seemed as though most people who took advantage of his services were going places they weren't really keen to go. He made efforts to put people at ease. Simon figured if they were going to be on the road, then they may as well make it a nice time. If people seemed open to talking, then he told them jokes, discussed the weather and football scores, and asked them questions about their children. As a job, it was okay.

He had only one more person to pick up in Maidstone, at an office block having something to do with the British Red Cross. He would return her to council housing on the other side of the city, where he'd collected her that morning. Favor was a tall girl with mocha coloured skin, a courageous refugee from the newly independent country of South Sudan. She had ridden with Simon twice before she had found the courage to make eye contact or answer his questions. The last time Simon had driven her, Favor had unexpectedly volunteered a small slice of her story. Her family was gone, she told Simon, and she had spent an entire year walking, sleeping on the ground and sometimes eating leaves to survive, in order to escape her native country.

She had left with her sister, Adeu, but her sister hadn't survived. They had traveled for five months, Favor said, when her sister died, during a dreadful storm. "She was taken by the curr-ant, and tin I saw a croco-die-all." Favor recounted the horror in her heavy accent, her expression never changing, though silent tears flowed down her brown face. The remainder of her journey to the UK remained a mystery, but the little he knew of her devastating history put Simon's own challenges in a new light. It was obvious that Favor had received some education; her English was good, and she was a bright girl. It seemed impossible to guess her age, but he knew she was young when she described her siblings' ages, and he learned she was the second child in the family. Today, Favor was wearing a bright orange shirt that appeared three sizes too large, with green trousers. Definitely not a local fashion look, but on her, it made sense. She possessed dignity in spades. More to the point, she was safe, fed, and alive, when other people in her life were no longer. Favor boarded the minibus with a quick glance and a shy smile.

"Good day, Favor?"

"Yes, quite good," Favor said in her light and breathy voice. She took a seat directly behind his driver's seat, implying that she was open to conversation. As he began to drive away, his phone shivered in his pocket. Since he was driving, Simon ignored the call.

"I have applied for seeveral jobs today," Favor said, her lips drawn back in a huge smile, featuring fat, bright, white teeth.

"Good on you, love. What do you hope to do?"

"I most enjoy chill-dren. To be what you call a chiwold-minder would be most enjoyed."

"Lots of people need help with their kiddies these days; I am sure you'll get something very soon. If you're working—if I don't see you again next week—good luck to you, Favor."

"And good luck to you, Mr. Simon Whiston. Summday I will come to you for a piece of furniture."

They chatted for a bit about her roommate. They grew quiet, each of them considering the future. Simon stopped at the traffic light alongside Favor's home. He looked on as the minibus door closed behind her. She turned and walked towards her flat, which he knew was a tiny efficiency, shared with another girl, in the corner of an old building. Humble indeed, but he knew that Favor would rise in the world. She just needed time and opportunity.

The traffic light changed, and Simon drove the two miles back towards the car park where the county housed its vehicles. He turned in the keys to the minibus, and made his way to his van. On the way, he found the call that had come earlier, from an unknown number here in Maidstone.

"Uncle Simon, it's Finley…" his nephew's voice began strongly, then faded. "Mum's been in an accident."

Simon paused outside his van, trying to understand the

implications. The phone was still pressed to his ear when it rang. Startled, he looked at the phone. It rang again, and he answered.

"Simon, it's Avalyn."

"Yes?"

"Don't worry, I am with Finley here at the hospital in Maidstone."

"My sister?"

"She's going to be just fine, Simon. Honestly."

"What's happened? Should I come there? Where is Peony?"

Avalyn's voice became a mumble. She was speaking to someone else. She came back on the line. "Peony's fine, she's with Lorna's friend, Emily. Why don't you come along to the hospital?"

As they rang off, anxiety gripped Simon's insides. He didn't know Avalyn that well. She could be lying. Even if Avalyn had wanted to tell him the worst, what could she say with Fin obviously standing by? His sister could be dead, and she'd want the news to be relayed to the children from their uncle. Perhaps he was the last to know the worst of the news.

The stress of not knowing immediately registered in Simon's body. He broke out in a sweat. His leg began to cramp; it would be painful to drive, but he must.

By the time Simon left his van in the car park and began walking towards the hospital, he had a better handle on his emotions. Simon shivered as his nose filled with an antiseptic smell and a few memories of his time as a patient intruded on his thoughts. Pressing the button for the lift, he ignored his surroundings as best he could. Everything would work out. The last several years—his illness, losing his wife, business, and home—had changed him; he was perhaps a little shell-shocked, still, and whereas he'd previously looked for silver linings, now he was a bit thunder shy. He was too prone to imagining the worst, because the worst had kept happening to him. But he needed to keep a steady head, even if he couldn't steady his walk, and take a positive view. His family deserved that, for taking him on. With a deep breath, he squared his shoulders, ignoring a prick of pain in his neck, got on the lift and went to find the lounge where

Avalyn was waiting with his nephew.

Finley's eyes had been trained on the lift, and he had a panicked expression on his face when the doors opened. The boy came striding towards him, stopping in front of Simon like a soldier awaiting orders.

Simon stepped forward and hugged the boy about the shoulders. "I am glad you're here to keep Avalyn company, Fin. You know how girls can be."

Chatting to him like one of the lads worked a treat. Finley grinned from ear to ear. They walked towards Avalyn, who was nursing a cup of coffee and standing in front of a darkening window. Simon felt some guilt for thinking she was beautiful, without yet knowing how his sister was. Simon gave Finley some money, and asked the boy to get them something to eat from the vending machine, which, according to a wall directory, was at the end of the corridor.

"How is she, really?"

Avalyn reached out for Simon's arm and gave it a reassuring squeeze. "She's in surgery, with a fractured tibia and badly broken ankle. But otherwise, she seems to be fine. Finley was struggling a bit with his composure when we spoke earlier."

"What happened?"

"We were told by a PC that she was leaving Miss Harrop's home in her car. A group of teenagers hit her, broadside. The PC said that their tyre marks indicated they were going quite fast, and the driver has been taken into custody."

"Lorna wasn't found at fault?"

"No. Lewis Hamilton wouldn't have dared go as fast on Parsley Road as that lot. Lorna couldn't have possibly seen them coming, especially given the hill coming up towards Miss Harrop's place."

"They'll be keeping her for a few days, won't they?"

"Yes. And it's doubtful we'll be able to see her for four, maybe five more hours, at least."

"I suppose I ought to take Fin home."

Finley, fists full of candy, joined the conversation. "I can't leave my mum."

"Wrong mate, you're coming home with me. You're going to eat something besides chocolate, have a bath, and go to bed. We'll talk to your mum on the phone when she's able. She's going to be in the operating theatre for a while, and then they'll have her on those lovely happy drugs. She'll not be thinking about much, you know. Except perhaps dreaming that she's eating lemon birthday cake from Charlotte's bakery."

"I suppose," Finley smiled. Simon knew his nephew was relieved to be able to surrender his stand, and the boy suddenly looked quite tired.

The trio turned towards the lift.

Chapter Twelve

NEARLY TWO WEEKS later, Avalyn walked into the Whiston's farmhouse, calling a hello to Lorna, who was stationed on the lounge sofa.

"How are you feeling this afternoon?"

Peony came running to greet Avalyn, reaching out both arms to be swept up and held.

"Very glad to see you!" Lorna said, laughing. Avalyn let Peony down and walked over to the sofa, and helped Lorna up on her crutches. They made their way slowly to the loo, Lorna pausing to rest from the effort.

"You're doing very well, Lorna."

"Because you wouldn't allow me not to excel as a patient, Avalyn," came Lorna's cheeky but playful reply.

It was true, Avalyn had to admit. What with living just across the way, and with Avalyn's passion for healing, not to mention her growing interest in Lorna's gorgeous brother, Avalyn had become a thrice-daily visitor to the Whiston home. She had lots of rules for Lorna, and was surprised to find that Lorna obeyed them to the letter. Avalyn was there to comfort Lorna and help her through the body-racking chills that came with the trauma her body had sustained in the car accident, to keep her organised with medications, and to insist that she be hydrated to protect her organs from the drugs that made Lorna's pain bearable. Avalyn's herbal tea helped calm Lorna, keeping frustration and tears at bay. It was Avalyn who'd shopped for large fleece pants that would fit over Lorna's plaster cast, brought home jumbo ice packs for swelling, plunged Lorna's other foot into an orthopaedic sock, and, rotating the schedule with Emily, they helped Lorna into the bath and onto her plastic garden chair that stood in the centre of the tub.

The results were worth their efforts. Lorna was improving daily. But other transformations were taking place at the farmhouse that, at first, weren't as obvious.

Avalyn took charge of the family's shopping, and made their meals. Gone were the fried foods, sausage rolls and copious bags of crisps that Lorna had served routinely. Not only was Avalyn cooking daily meals, she also made double portions, filling the deep freeze with healthy dinners that would be close to hand when Lorna was back on her feet.

For Avalyn's part, she loved cooking. Preparing meals for herself oftentimes seemed not worth the effort. Having a family—especially the children, who were not in the least fussy—to cook for had been one of the most satisfying joys that she'd known in a long time.

With Lorna settled back on the sofa and Peony given a fresh book to colour, Avalyn turned to her work in the kitchen. Roasted chicken was a family favourite. She uncovered a loaf of walnut-honey bread that she'd baked at her cottage and sliced it, prepared a fresh salad, and an easy recipe of red pepper, broccoli and cauliflower dressed with citrus sauce. Afters were slices of cheese and sweet apples.

Simon and Finley came through the door just as Avalyn was finishing up. Simon came up behind her, encircling her in his arms as she turned the vegetables into a serving dish.

"Hmm, mouth-watering," he whispered into her neck. Avalyn smiled and said, "Yes, this family does appreciate home cooking."

"You know I was talking about you," Simon caressed her neck. "Is there anything I can do to help?"

"Yes, help Peony wash her hands, and bring Lorna to the table, if you would."

"Yes, of course. Come along, Sweet Pea."

Throughout the meal, Avalyn was aware of Finley's restlessness. He was quieter than usual, and swung his legs under the table, seemingly impatient for something. Although she was deepening her relationship with the Whiston family, Avalyn kept her place and her observation to herself. But Lorna had apparently noticed, too.

"Out with it, Fin," his mother demanded, as Avalyn cleared the dishes for pudding.

Finley, in turn, grinned at his uncle.

"Go on, then," Simon said.

"We've been working very hard, out in the garage. And we've finished restoring the motorbike that my Grandfather Oakley had left there."

"Well done, my clever boy," Lorna said, smiling broadly at her son.

Simon said that Fin had truly done work, not just watched as some children his age might do. Lorna and Avalyn could read between the lines, knowing that Finley had often been Simon's hands, on those days when Simon's joints ached too badly to use the tools.

"As soon as I get home from school tomorrow, we're going for a ride," Finley said. "It was too dark when we finished today."

"How lovely," Avalyn said. "I'll want to get some snaps to capture the moment, before the pair of you ride off into the sunset."

"Avalyn, would you mind to print those when you do?" Lorna asked her. "I'd like to send them to Mum in my next letter. She may even remember the motorcycle and be able to give you some history, Fin."

"I go, too," Peony said, while nailing her Uncle Simon with a look. It was obvious that she'd quickly learned her uncle was a pushover.

"Gemma doesn't have a helmet," Simon replied. Peony considered this. Simon supposed that when they fired up the noisy motorcycle that she would no longer be interested.

"There's more," Fin said. "We're going to auction the motorcycle at the fete, and make you rich, Mum."

Avalyn could see that Lorna was too touched to speak. Lorna teared up, and reached out her hands. Fin slipped from his chair, carefully walked around her leg, which was propped up to the side of the table, and came into his mother's embrace. Avalyn's heart squeezed and she felt that she could cry, too. It would be lovely to have children, especially young children, because Lorna's nine-year old son wasn't yet too grown up to allow his mum to hold him for a little.

After getting the children off to bed, and Lorna settled for the night, Simon walked Avalyn home.

"You've been amazing to all of us since Lorna's accident," he said, holding her hand and coming up to the door of her cottage with her. "I don't know where we'd be without you."

Avalyn turned and put her free hand into his hair, which he'd neglected to get cut recently. "I don't know where I'd be without you. All of you. I was so lonely, Simon. You, Lorna, and the children have become sort of like my adopted family. It's been my pleasure to help, and, the truth is, I don't like to think of what I'll do when Lorna is well and I am no longer needed."

Still holding her hand, Simon gently bent her arm behind her waist, and stepped in close. His other hand cupped her jaw and lifted her face to his. He kissed her, and she melted against him. "Don't worry, baby," Simon said, looking into her eyes. "You'll never be on your own again."

Chapter Thirteen

LORNA LONGED TO leave the sofa. Everyone was lovely, Emily and Avalyn were minding the children, cooking meals, and doing laundry. Simon was especially sweet, and she realised that he'd changed in this regard, no doubt due to his own physical suffering. Lorna smiled, remembering him last evening, doing the washing up and flirting with Avalyn. Tonight as he picked up the children's toys, he had done so seemingly without pain. She asked him about it.

"You appear to be feeling better."

"I am. I suppose you'll think me ridiculous, but I haven't wanted to say anything. Don't want to jinx myself. But it feels good to move again."

"Yes, I'd like a little of that feeling, now. This bum leg has given me a new appreciation for what you must've been going through, Simon. Besides being enormous right before the children were born, I've never had to slow down, or been not able to do anything, ever in my life. It's awful, really."

What Lorna had also come to understand is how it felt to be quickly running out of money, and not be able to rely on your own labour to get the bills paid. Surely, it must have been devastating to her brother to lose everything financially. She better understood why her brother had surrendered his home to Dominique. Probably, he wouldn't have been able to keep it running and pay the taxes anyway, so why not just give it to his wife, who was making a rather good salary. If they had sold in the market that favoured buyers several years ago, a good deal of money may have been lost. It made sense to her, now.

Simon ran a hand along the back of his neck. It was a thoughtful gesture that Lorna remembered of their father, but she was thankful that her brother wasn't anything like him otherwise, except his brilliance at building and fixing things.

"I think that's the best bit," Simon replied. "I thought for a long time that I'd never feel better. There wasn't going to be a particular day for me when everything is much better, as you'll have when they remove your cast. I don't mind telling you I shed more than a few tears, thinking of being trapped in a body full of pain for the rest of my life."

He came and slowly sat down on Lorna's sofa. He wore a serious expression.

"What?"

"I've wondered if maybe I could build a bench for the village green. Have it done in a couple of weeks, in time for the fete. I know it would cost the village some money, and I don't know if they're interested. And, for my part, there's none to be made, I am volunteering my work. But for some reason, its something I want to do."

"That's lovely, Simon, honestly. I think you ought to make the bench, if you can."

Her brother beamed. "My body seems like it would cooperate. And if Fin was on hand, that would give me confidence that I wouldn't waste the wood and supplies. Between Fin and me, I am quite certain we'd have a bench to show for it."

Lorna's mobile rang. She looked at Simon with wide-eyes. "It's Hugo!"

Grinning, Simon promptly left the room.

"Hello?"

"You haven't returned my calls. And you haven't sent me a bill for that hard slog at Auntie's house. Have you given up?"

"No, not in the way that you mean, but I have suffered a setback. I am so sorry, Hugo, I suppose I should have rung you up and told you. There never seemed to be a good time."

"Told me what, exactly?"

She explained about leaving Miss Harrop's and ending up in hospital with a broken leg from a car crash with speeding teenagers.

Hugo expressed his shock and sympathy. "Lorna, I am so very sorry. Are you managing okay with the children?"

"Yes. Of course, Simon's been a great help, and my friend, Emily, whom you met when you popped in that day. She's been wonderful. And our neighbour, Avalyn."

"Avalyn? That couldn't be Avalyn Smith, surely? It's an unusual enough name, but doubtful…"

"Yes! That *is* her name. Do you know her?" The line was quiet. "Hugo, are you there?"

"Look, Lorna, I suppose there's no getting around it. Avalyn and I dated. Funny thing, it was I who first brought her to Burleigh Cross."

Hugo ran on, but Lorna was no longer listening. Had she ever mentioned Hugo's name to Avalyn? She didn't think she had. So, it wasn't as though Avalyn was keeping them in the dark. But all the same, it was an odd coincidence. How could one person be Hugo's ex-girlfriend, Lorna's friend, and her brother's girlfriend? It sounded like the worst sort of TV drama. Perhaps, Lorna thought, it was a sort of sign that Avalyn wasn't right for Simon after all. Lorna hardly knew Avalyn, yet the woman practically had the running of her house.

Maybe it was time for a change that was inevitable, and what Lorna felt was nothing to do with Hugo and Avalyn's relationship, or Avalyn's current relationship with Simon. It was just time that she ought to stop allowing the woman to work so hard, cleaning their home and cooking all of their meals. Surely, Lorna had been acting quite spoilt. And surely, they could manage on their own.

"Lorna, you've gone quiet," Hugo was saying. "And I'm afraid I've tired you out, love. I ought to let you rest. Not to mention, they've probably got you on a few painkillers, eh? Not that you sounded inappropriate or anything."

Lorna imagined Hugo and Avalyn together, dressed up, both of them tall and looking smashing. Her leg ached and she felt dumpy at best. Perhaps Hugo wasn't the man of her dreams, and it was terribly likely, she wasn't the woman of his. True, he'd shown concern and asked questions, yet she felt as though, given the right circumstances, he and Avalyn may have a laugh about her and Simon falling so quickly for the pair of them. The thought made her go off him. She felt too tired at the moment to continue.

"Yes, I think I ought to rest, Hugo. Thank you for calling. I am sorry I haven't been in touch." There was one thing she was sure of. "I haven't changed my mind about cleaning your aunt's cottage, but I understand if you wouldn't want to wait on me. If you hired on someone else, you could certainly have sold by the time I've finished recovering."

"No, no, I wouldn't think of it," Hugo assured her. Admittedly, that was decent of him. And Avalyn was a lovely woman. Why should it matter that they'd been together? Lorna had two children with other blokes, so who was she to throw stones? Like Hugo'd said, these conflicting emotions must have something to do with medication.

It was another mild, early September day. The sunshine slanted through the window and warmed her as she waited for Emily. Lorna wished she could at least offer her friend a hot cuppa when she came in. They had placed some dreadful hardware in her leg, and so hobbling about, even the few feet she'd have to go to put the kettle on, was quite an undertaking. Finally, she heard Emily's car in the drive. Two car doors slamming, the first for Emily, and the second came after Emily had taken baby Bethany from her car seat. Peony had heard them, too, and came running from the bathroom before Uncle Simon could put her top on.

"Peony!" Lorna's brother came flying around the corner. "You're not topped off, pet."

"Look at you, you're running, Simon! No more moving like an

ancient."

He grinned as he popped Peony's fuchsia shirt over her head, and she ran to greet Emily.

"Hi Emily," Simon said, as Lorna's friend put a hand on Peony's shoulder to return a leg hug. "I'll be off, then. You girls have fun."

"Where's he headed?" Emily asked.

"Probably to see someone in the village. Great news, Em. Simon has a carpentry project in mind." Lorna told Emily about the bench Simon wanted to build for the village green, and how at least one member of the council had spoken to Simon over the telephone and seemed agreeable.

Emily smiled. "It's so good to see him doing so well. He certainly has come a long way in a short while. I think having family around is good for him, and I am sure Avalyn has helped as well."

"About her," Lorna began.

"Mummy, I want to play outside," Peony interrupted.

"Let's give her a few minutes fresh air," Lorna said, "and then we can talk."

It seemed an eternity, waiting again for Emily, Peony, and the baby to come back inside. Lorna began to feel guilty about the strange distrust she'd had of Avalyn. Emily was right; Simon was in high spirits, relaxed, and much healthier in a matter of weeks, and Avalyn had certainly played a role.

Emily came inside, unbundling Bethany while Peony wriggled out of her coat. Peony went to retrieve Gemma and a fairy doll, whose name, for reasons only fully appreciated by Peony, was "Nice."

Emily came over to the chair by Lorna's sofa and sat upon it with Bethany in her arms. "Alright, so what was it you were about to say? Something about Avalyn?"

Lorna let a sigh escape her lips. "I feel awful telling you, but I've got to tell someone."

Emily laughed. "Well, go on then."

"Lots of news. Firstly, I heard from Hugo yesterday, wondering why I'd gone missing."

"Thrilling!"

"Yes, I know. He's been travelling for work. I told him about the accident and he was very sympathetic, asked loads of questions, and intends to let me carry on cleaning up old Miss Harrop's house as soon as I can manage."

"Oh, Lorna, how fabulous!" Emily said, sitting her pretty baby on her lap and supporting Bethany's back with her hand. Lorna knew that Bethany would be as pretty as Emily when she grew up, with the same dark hair and eyes. She smiled at Emily, and, knowing Lorna in and out, Emily smiled back and said, "Thank you."

"And so Hugo was asking how I am managing, and of course I told him about how you, Simon, and Avalyn have been such stars. And he said, '*Avalyn Smith?*'"

At this, Emily's jaw dropped, and Lorna felt a bit of satisfaction. It *did* matter.

"Truly! And he went on to say that they'd *dated*, and it was *he* who brought her to visit the village at some point—I guess my mind wandered at that part of his story. It seems unlikely that they were here to visit his aunt, but who knows about people?"

"Indeed. How completely unexpected."

Lorna said, "Isn't it, just?"

Emily nodded.

"Well, is that *all*?" Lorna asked.

"What'd you mean?"

Lorna sighed. Emily's half-hearted response was disappointing.

"It's completely unexpected, yes. But don't you think it's somehow more than that? It's changed *everything*, Em!"

Emily laughed. That was disappointing as well. "What are you on about? Whatever do you mean, 'it's changed everything'?"

Lorna frowned, thinking where to start. "I don't feel the same about Avalyn, now. I am not even sure that I like her for Simon."

Emily rolled her eyes.

"What?"

"Lorna, you didn't like Miss Harrop, either. Or Hugo, for that matter. Look where that got you. Now you're cleaning the bloody woman's house and wondering if he's boyfriend material."

"You never curse."

"Sorry to let you down."

"You didn't. It just makes me feel worse when you're not Emily the Good, to my Lorna the Bad."

"You're not bad. You're just prone to being a little sensitive. A bit suspicious as well."

Lorna wanted to stride purposefully about the room, but she was restricted to the sofa. "You were really surprised that Avalyn and Hugo dated. Why be surprised if it just really doesn't matter? You seemed, just for a tick, a bit sensitive and suspicious, too, am I correct?"

Emily smiled, but then pulled her contemplating face. She always tried to see Lorna's side, and for that, Lorna loved her. Lorna waited patiently. This was getting to the real truth of things and what they meant. Hopefully.

"Do you think this would make any difference to Simon?" Emily asked. "Surely, you've been thinking about telling him that Avalyn dated Hugo. What do you imagine he'll say?"

This somehow wasn't the angle she'd thought Emily would take, but she tried to answer thoughtfully. "Yes, I have done. And I imagine that he wouldn't mind. I think he would have a moment of considering it an odd coincidence, but he likes Hugo well enough, and so I don't think he'd think much else about it."

Emily hugged Bethany and kissed the top of her head. "If I am honest, Lorna, we don't actually know if Hugo has a potentially serious interest in you."

"Thanks a lot for cutting right to the quick, Emily."

"Oh, come along now. Look, what doesn't make sense to me is why Avalyn has heard you speak of cleaning Miss Harrop's house so many times, and yet she never seemed to connect the name to her ex-boyfriend."

That was the bit Lorna had waited for. Once again, Emily had clarified what mattered.

Chapter Fourteen

SIMON FINISHED UNLOADING the wood from his van into the workshop. His muscles ached from use, which wasn't the same as the sharp pain he had thought he'd never be without. He had drawn up his plans for the bench, took them to the council meeting, and gained enthusiastic approval. All of his materials were ready. Finley was at school, and Simon was anxious to see how he could get on without his nephew's help.

As he drew on his worn, leather work gloves, Simon couldn't stifle a grin from spreading across his face. The wood lay solid in his hands, and he could move about as he pleased with no pain, pressure, or problem. The high windows of the workshop streamed with sunshine, and the fragrance of cut wood filled the air. Birds sat high on the rafters, twittering at each other and giving voice to the contentment he felt. He settled into constructing the frame for the bench. After a bit, his mind wandered. Perhaps it wasn't impossible to go back to crafting furniture. He considered working for someone else, but that brought a twinge of apprehension. There were always extra hours and deadlines to be met. He felt he couldn't take the pressure of letting someone down, just in case his body wouldn't cooperate again. The doctors had said that stress was an enemy to his health.

So, it was possibly a matter of going back into business for himself; starting small, working carefully, getting plenty of rest, and taking care of himself. When he thought about living well, Avalyn invariably sprung to mind. She inspired him, made him laugh, and helped him believe anything was possible. And what an amazing cook she was. He knew there must be something to the diet aspect of managing his condition, because he'd realised he felt a little better after Lorna stopped buying the fizzy drinks he used to nurse all day long. He'd continued to improve when Avalyn began cooking for them. Not to mention, family life seemed to be part of the cure; Lorna's support gave him confidence and the children had taught him how to laugh again. His doctor hadn't specifically prescribed any of these relationship changes in his life, but they were working far more powerfully on his health than any medication had done.

Simon smiled to himself. Avalyn was so beautiful. There was something about a beautiful woman that made him want to create something for her. Not that the bench would go in her garden, but her beauty, kindness, and her femininity spurred him on to be a part of the life and love happening in the world around him. She brought out his best.

Simon couldn't suppress another smile. Here he was, shavings on his shoes again, smelling the deep, spicy scent of fresh timber, and waxing romantic about a girl. Life was good.

Lorna woke in the middle of the night, having to go to the loo. She lay for a few minutes looking through her window at the moon, majestically shining from a fold of thick grey clouds, willing herself to be able to fall back asleep. No such luck. Passing water in the bedpan was beyond disgusting and she'd refused to use the one they sent home with her from hospital. She swung her now-booted, bum leg towards the floor, stuffed her stick beneath the opposite arm, and struggled upwards. She was up on her good foot, holding steady, but with a burning brain and a feeling that she was going to faint. She took a deep breath, and waited for the sensation to subside.

Mercifully, it did.

Now to manoeuver herself across her bedroom, and the long walk to the bathroom. Her conscience told her she shouldn't attempt it, but now that her body sensed relief was not far off, she *must* go. She hobbled towards the end of her bed. She moved with slow, well-planned efforts, holding on to the foot of her antique brass bedstead. She managed the connecting distance between her bed and the doorway, and then something went pear shaped. In one horrifying moment she was lying on the floor, feeling warm liquid on the side of her body, and excruciating pain in her broken ankle. Loud noise reverberated in her ears. She realised it was a yelp she let out as she fell. No doubt she'd alarmed her children and woken them from their deep sleep.

Simon was on the stairs, she heard him clomp up three at a time. He found her in the doorway and attempted to pick her up in the dark, not realising he was standing on a lock of her hair.

"Owl! Put me down!"

"Sorry. You're right, you shouldn't be moved till we see everything's okay."

He flipped on the light and it was blinding, like the lamp that had hovered above her in the operating theatre. She feared she'd be headed back for another surgery. It was enough to make her feel faint again.

She started to weep. "Oh, I am bleeding, I must have broken my ankle again, or in another place! Look at it!"

Her brother was on his knees, leaning beside her. Lorna felt him remove the boot that had shifted, and gently squeeze her ankle. He failed to realise what was important—that she was going to need surgery all over again.

"Don't you care? This bleeding means the surgery's no good, now. Oh, I can't bear it, I swear I can't!" She couldn't hold back her tears, whatever her poor children might be overhearing.

"No, love. You're fine."

"But—"

"Well, you've peed, haven't you."

"What? Oh."

"Rest there a bit, and I'll get a towel from the bath."
"Are the children awake?"
"Somehow, no."

The next morning Lorna was quite under the weather. Falling, and the corresponding fear and humiliation that came with the tumble, had squashed her spirits.

Her mobile rang. It was Hugo. "I didn't think your social calendar would be very full, so I am taking the liberty of popping in," he said. Suddenly the earth was spinning properly on its axis.

"Oh, Hugo, how sweet. Mind you, I am not very glamorous, and you'll have to let yourself in, but I am so excited that you're coming to visit."

"I am just over the bridge. See you soon."

Earlier she'd put on a little lipstick and stroke of mascara, trying to help herself feel better. She was grateful for that little grace now. Finley was at school, Emily had collected Peony for a couple of hours for the village playgroup. Simon was off to Maidstone to buy some sort of stain or other for the council to approve for the bench, so she and Hugo would be quite alone.

She heard his car pull in from the lane and her heart danced. A busy man like Hugo would be missed at the office; she knew his coming from London to see her was a sacrifice of time and effort. She heard his feet crunch across the drive, step onto the porch, and a moment later he materialised, looking even more handsome than she remembered.

He came bearing gifts.

"Hello Hugo! Oh my, you've brought pressies. Would you like tea or something? I am sorry you'll have to help yourself."

"No. We've got lunch plans."

"What? Honestly, I can't hobble about very well. Are you sure you want to go out?"

Afraid of disturbing her leg, Hugo had laid down some packages and was pushing a chair closer to where Lorna sat on the sofa.

"For you," he said, handing her a box of chocolates swathed in satin.

"Oh, they look divine. Is this what you meant when you mentioned lunch? Because I could manage to eat quite a few of these."

"No, you mustn't spoil your appetite. Here's another."

Lorna took a beautifully wrapped present from his hands, noticing that he smelled rather delicious. Expensive, if that was a scent. Today he wasn't in a suit, but Hugo still looked a million in a patterned shirt, suede jacket and dark jeans.

She loosened the floral paper from the box.

And heard the door open.

It was Avalyn.

Lorna's temper spiked. "Hello, Avalyn—what are you doing here?"

Her neighbour, accustomed to coming and going at all hours to bring meals, help mind the children, or lend a hand to Lorna with bathing or to give her tea, was rather too stunned to make a reply. Lorna saw Avalyn's eyes meet Hugo's.

Lorna couldn't bear it. "Well, I suppose you two know each other. Or, rather, you did."

Hugo stood and crossed the room. Away from Lorna. Towards Avalyn.

He said something to her in a voice that Lorna couldn't hear. Lovely. *Now they were going to have a private chat in her kitchen?*

Lorna cursed her broken leg, let the gift box slide from her hand and come to the floor, and realised that she couldn't even leave the room to give these people their privacy. Another vehicle was in the drive. Good, Lorna thought, perhaps Simon can join the fray. May as well get as many people involved in this ridiculous party as possible.

Only it wasn't her brother. Lorna heard a curt knock on the door. Avalyn stepped aside, *thanks for that much*, Lorna thought, and let Hugo open the door. Fantastically, in came a pair of men along with a woman, dressed in black and white. The men carried what appeared to be domes made of stainless steel, the woman had a huge bouquet of white lilies interspersed with fall foliage and a small stack of black linen. As the men walked back through the open door, the woman began to dress the kitchen table in black linens. Through the open kitchen door, Lorna heard yet another vehicle drove up.

In addition to a catered lunch, Simon arrived.

Some confused minutes later, Lorna sat with her leg propped up alongside the table, helped, as usual, by her brother and Avalyn. Opposite her sat Hugo, chatting with Simon about people they knew from the village, catching up on the news in Chelsea, where Simon had lived and Hugo had close mates. As it happened, the caterers were equipped to handle additional diners, as Hugo hadn't known if either of the children, Emily, or Simon may unexpectedly be in the house. Thus plates were set for Simon and Avalyn. The lunch consisted of a soup with cream decoratively swirled onto its surface, followed by creative, colorful little towers of food, standing in moats of sauce. Lorna couldn't have said what the food actually was, and didn't really care to know.

What she did know was one of the best surprises of her life had just been spoilt, and she was feeling rather sorry for herself. The only person who hadn't come bursting through the door was her friend, Emily, bringing Peony home, and Lorna wished for them. Not only so that Emily could witness this farce with her own eyes and save Lorna lots of time explaining just how awful it all was, but also Lorna would very much like her friend to help her into bed, close the door, and leave her in peace. She would definitely treat herself to a good cry, and if Em could manage bringing the box of chocs up to Lorna's bedroom more's the better.

Since escape eluded her at present, Lorna's thoughts wondered to Avalyn. What had Hugo said to her in the kitchen? She looked at Avalyn, wondering. Avalyn must have felt Lorna's gaze, because she suddenly turned to her. Avalyn instantly smiled, and said, "Isn't this a treat?"

Yes, and how many lunches like this one have you eaten with Hugo? Lorna wanted to ask. She nodded and forced the corners of her lips to rise at Hugo's ex-girlfriend. Lorna hadn't meant to go on staring, but she was a bit foggy on medication, and Avalyn caught her out. Lorna tried to assume an air of graciousness and pleasure. She wanted to be above these wretched thoughts swirling around in her mind, but it was obvious that her attempts were in vain when Avalyn asked, "You're in a lot of pain?"

"No." *I must have a face like thunder, trying to endure this surprise double date,* Lorna thought. Perhaps since Em hadn't shown up, Avalyn could instead be her ticket upstairs to bed, with the chocs. She no longer cared if Avalyn and Hugo were going to have further private conversation.

Wait, Lorna reasoned, *that meant it would be best to have Simon take me up. Yes, why not—give the lovers their moment over lunch and wine. Simon would return and see for himself. How Hugo and Avalyn had been having them on. Maybe they still dated each other, for all she and Simon knew.*

She interrupted someone's conversation. "Simon, would you take me upstairs?"

"Yes, of course, love. Aren't you feeling well?"

"Not particularly. Thank you so very much, Hugo. So very sorry, I need to go and have a lie down. Must be all of the excitement."

With some satisfaction, she saw that Hugo was quite embarrassed. He was realising, Lorna guessed, that he hadn't been paying her any attention; the invalid he'd come to see, who'd gotten harmed trying to help out his dear ole auntie. Hugo spouted on for a moment about being let down Lorna wouldn't have pudding with them, and how he'd return to see her, soon.

To see me—or her?

"Can I do anything to help?" Avalyn asked.

"If you'd hand Simon the gifts that Hugo brought, I'd like to have them with me," Lorna said, in a voice dripping with treacle.

"Of course," Avalyn said, scuttling off to gather the pair of boxes from the sofa and the floor. She tucked them under Simon's free arm as brother and sister made their slow journey up the stairs.

"Be back in a tick," Simon called over his shoulder. *Yes, and you would be in a hurry if you knew what kind of chat they'll get up to when we're out of earshot,* thought Lorna.

Simon settled her on the bed, and placed the gifts from Hugo beside her. He helped her elevate her leg just so. Then he walked to the other side of the bed and sat down.

"What's going on, then?"

Lorna feigned indignation. "What d'you mean?"

"Oh, come on, Lorna. We were out of touch for years, I know, but this is you acting like you did as a child. When someone hurts your feelings, you're off like a rabbit. You're hiding. And punishing people by walking out."

"You think I am 'punishing' Hugo, do you? Or Avalyn? Well, I am sorry if I've mistreated your lovely friends. And, for the record, Simon, when it comes to relationships, I am not the one who walks out."

"You know I didn't mean that sort of walking out. Are you jealous because Hugo was talking too much with me? That's my fault, you know, he was just being polite. I am the one who's curious about how the old neighbourhood has gotten along fine without me. I probably was boring him to tears. I am sorry, Sis. I didn't mean to ruin his visit."

He really was quite decent as brothers went. She reached out and batted him with the back of her hand, as though shooing a ladybird. A hug might have been nice, but now that she'd actually come up the stairs, her leg really was aching.

"Alright, I can see you're going to be chatting about this to Emily instead of me," he said with a smile. "I'll check on you when they've gone."

"Thanks, Simon. I'll have a kip and feel much better by the time the kiddies come home."

Lorna couldn't sleep. Instead, she did a lot of thinking. Turning things over in her mind hadn't yielded anything but more agitation when she heard the kitchen door open and close behind their guests. She'd give a tenner to be able to spring up from bed, dash across to the front of the house, peer out the nursery window, and spy on Hugo and Avalyn as they were leaving, to see if they were chatting, or, worse, touching each other in some way.

Chapter Fifteen

THE BENCH FOR the village green was finished. Finley helped his Uncle Simon to apply the stain, and the boy was doing a careful job.

"You're as good a painter as you are a mechanic," he told Finley, who grinned at the compliment.

"It just takes a little slowing down to stop it being messy, right?"

"Yes, that's right. So, if I make something else, are you going to help me?"

"Yeah. But I wish you wouldn't get on while I am at school. I missed most of this."

Simon laughed. "I didn't think it was that intriguing."

Finley stroked on the last of the stain, and his uncle helped him with cleaning the brushes and putting the lid back on the tin. They walked to the farmhouse.

Lorna was in the kitchen, shoving something frozen into the oven.

"What are you doing on your feet? Didn't you learn your lesson falling over the end of your bed the other night?" Simon scolded, while supportively holding out his arm at the same time. "If there's something in particular you wanted for tea then you could've asked me for help."

She straightened up and crossed her arms. "I can get the tea on by myself. In fact, there's no reason to have meals brought around all of the time."

"What are you saying?"

"I am saying, Simon, that we can manage on our own."

"But Avalyn's been a wonderful help. How do you think she'll feel, when she comes in today—possibly carrying in a homemade pie, mind you—and finds you've popped something in to cook from a cardboard box you found in the deep freeze? Especially when she's left a store of meals in there?"

"She won't be coming." Lorna wanted to shuffle back to the sofa on her brother's arm, but Simon had forgotten they were meant to be moving.

"Is she busy at the clinic?"

"Busy at the clinic? You say that as though she's a *real* doctor or other. No, I rang her and told her not to come."

"Why?"

"Because I don't want her in *my* house any more. I don't need her to feed my children."

"Is this something to do with Hugo's visit yesterday?" He withdrew his arm, and she hopped twice on her good foot before reaching a kitchen chair.

"Do you want me to fall simply because I don't like your witchy girlfriend?"

Simon gave Finley a look that said, "Go." The boy went, knowing there was about to be a row. Finley was a conscientious brother, and Simon knew that he'd collect Peony on his way out of the room and keep her occupied for a few minutes.

"Why did you ring her and tell her to stop coming? What did you say to her?"

"What's it to you if I don't want her cooking meals for my family any more? You don't know what it's like, or you wouldn't fuss. It takes hours to come up with meals like that, going to the shops and cooking and helping with the cleaning up. It's not her responsibility."

"But she enjoys it, and enjoys being here. And do tell me if you were horribly rude."

"Of course I was not horribly rude, I simply said we could manage."

"Lorna, why? She's been nothing but kind to us."

"Perhaps that's exactly why. She doesn't have to go on permanently, being rather slavish and over-the-top."

Simon said nothing. Lorna was obviously seething despite the cool face she was wearing.

"Excuse me, Simon, but why are you taking up her side? Haven't I been kind to you? Haven't I opened my home to you? Who else would do that?"

"Do you really think Avalyn wouldn't?"

"Perfect. You can go live with her, then. She can cook three-a-day for you. Go on. Be happy with yourselves."

Simon wanted to pack his clothes and go. Nothing, in fact, could be more appealing. He imagined Avalyn in the kitchen as he came in from work. The fire would be dancing in the grate, throwing warming light throughout the cottage. He'd open a bottle of wine.

But he'd be able to see his sister's house from Avalyn's window. And he knew that moving out after having a relationship destroying row with his sister would hurt Finley and Peony deeply. Not to mention, Avalyn hadn't actually asked him to come live with her.

"No."

Lorna had hobbled to the sofa. She sat down before she replied. "What do you mean, 'no'? In case you're not clear, I've just tossed you out. You've no choice but to go."

"Then you'll have to call the police and have me removed. Who's the constable 'round Burleigh? Is it still Matthew Parker? We used to play rugger together. I expect he'll be thrilled to see me."

He came to sit down by his sister. For a person who'd so casually levered power over her brother she looked more than miserable. "You can tell PC Parker that Mum owns the house, and as the oldest I have no legal right to be here. That ought to convince him."

"I'll make a report of domestic violence. You let go of me in the kitchen."

"Despite how much I find you maddening, you're my sister. I love being part of Fin and Peony's lives, and even yours. Even though I am just your previously estranged brother, I am going to be the bloke who doesn't leave. Not just yet, anyway, and certainly not because you're being rather annoying."

"Oh sod off, Simon." Lorna wiped a few tears away with the sleeve of her bathrobe. This was the first day she hadn't dressed since being released from hospital. He imagined it was because Avalyn hadn't been allowed to come this morning, and his sister had had all she could do to manage Peony, meals, and housework on her own.

"You're going to hear me out, Lorna. You see, I am a bit more of the grateful sort than I was a few years ago. I've been without family, and realised I always would be, unless you and I could work things out. What's more, I am also slightly more aware that the whole world doesn't revolve around me, or my business. I admit, this revelation came easier when I no longer had a business. But I do have you, and my nephew and niece. And Mum, if she ever comes back to England. So I am trying not to cock everything up."

"Right. You've succeeded in making me feel guilty. I won't call the coppers to make you go. Leave me alone."

"No."

"You're doing my head in, Simon. You're like a two-year-old."

"No."

She laughed, and Simon knew the worst was over.

"Lorna."

"What now?"

"Shall I call Avalyn?"

"*No.*"

"But you do realise you hadn't turned on the oven. We're likely to starve."

"I told you. I don't want her in my house."

"Tell me why."

"I can't talk about it. I'll cry. And what's worse, I am not sure *why.*"

Simon slipped his arm around her shoulders and hugged her gently. Then he kissed the top of her head, as he did with Peony.

"I'll go to the village for take-away. We'll sort this later."

Simon wasn't sure what he'd say to Avalyn, but he hoped if he gave Lorna a few days of trying to do everything herself, then she'd be more than willing to have Avalyn's help again.

Chapter Sixteen

AVALYN LAY ON the floor by her dog. She wasn't sure what time it was, but she'd been unable to sleep. Gus was snoring away on the rug by her bedside. She had felt cold, then too warm, and had rumpled the bedclothes with her thrashing about. She'd finally given up and decided to cuddle up with Gus for a few minutes. The hard stone floor of the cottage actually felt good. Solid. The tears that she'd held back came spilling into Gus's fur. Then she got a dog hair in her eye, and that made it worse, but at least crying would help flush it out.

Lorna could be spiteful, but Avalyn liked her. At least one knew where they stood. Avalyn sensed the real reason Lorna was upset had little to do with her. It wasn't personal. Unfortunately, it felt very personal at the moment, as Lorna had succeeded in separating her from Simon. For this evening, and perhaps for always.

Simon hadn't bothered to ring or drop by. He surely knew that his sister had forbidden her to come to the house, bearing meat pie or not, and seemingly he had done nothing. His affections were with his sister, his loyalty with the sibling who gave him shelter, and his niece and nephew, whom he adored.

And why should his loyalty be with me, Avalyn reasoned. They'd had only one date. Since he came for dinner, he had not reciprocated. Despite sweet words and looks of love, he hadn't actually made a move towards keeping the relationship going.

But they had been together most nights for weeks, a knocked together family around Lorna's kitchen table. He had given Avalyn most of his meagre cheque to pay for the food that she prepared for them all. How could she imagine Simon could afford to take her out on dates? He had demands on his time, as well. Should he stop tutoring Finley with his maths, minding Peony, and helping his sister run their household, simply because Avalyn craved his attention?

She felt guilty. But she still wished he would ring.

The next morning at the Whistons' farmhouse, Peony was sitting by her uncle at the breakfast table, finishing her cereal. "Mummy, when's Avil coming back?"

"I was wondering the same thing, Peony," Simon said, garnering a warning look from his sister.

"Finish your breakfast, Peony, and then we'll work on your numbers and do Barnaby Bear on the computer."

Simon saw Lorna wiggling the toes of her propped up foot. She looked exhausted. Maybe she would talk. Simon slid over to the chair closest to her. "There's something you're not telling me."

"Alright. My friend, and your friend, were an item," Lorna said, coding the message in front of Peony.

Simon considered this. "Really?"

"Yes."

"When?"

"I don't know."

He didn't really see the significance. While it was sort of odd that Avalyn hadn't mentioned it, he hardly thought it sinister. "And the problem is?"

"Don't you think it's odd that somehow we've only just found out?"

"I dunno. You may think it's even odder that I've hardly told Ava —*my friend*—anything about my previous relationships, except my marriage, in broad strokes."

Lorna didn't answer.
Simon tried again. "I've already asked you. What's the problem?"
"I just feel like we're both being played somehow."
"Care to explain that?"
"I can't."
"Based on this rather insignificant feeling, I am assuming you'll allow me to invite *my friend* back?"
"No."
"Lorna."
"I am sorry, Simon."
"Mummy, I was done."
"Okay, Peony." To Simon, she said, "Will you help me to the sofa, or are you going to retaliate?"
"Don't be daft. And pay attention, Mummy, as you're about to squash Gemma with your stick."

Avalyn worked through the morning updating her patient charts. Her practice was slowly picking up, and this afternoon she had eight appointments. She was close to needing an assistant, which was rather exciting progress.
Last night, she'd been making excuses for Simon. This morning, she woke up *angry*.
But no time to spare for thinking about another bloke who'd let her down. A cup of tea would help the task along, and although she had no plans for this evening, she didn't want to spend it at the clinic. She stepped into her small kitchen at the rear of the office space, filled the electric kettle, and flipped the switch. Her mobile rang. Curiously, it was Hugo.
"Avalyn, it's eleven," Hugo said. "Having tea, aren't you?"
Caught in the act of being predictable, she had to laugh. "Of course."
"Do you have time for a little chat?"
Unable to chat with a boyfriend of her own, why not talk to Lorna's?
"Sure, Hugo."

Simon drove to the village and had a nice chinwag with several council members. They were very pleased with the bench, which his neighbour, Mr. Pugh, along with his son, Pauley, had delivered to its final resting place at the edge of the village green. Then he made his way to Avalyn's office.

He stepped in quietly. She didn't have a receptionist yet, and he didn't want to interrupt should she have a client at the moment. He stood in reception, listening for sounds of an appointment in progress. Instead, he could hear Avalyn's voice drifting from the small kitchenette at the back of the office space. She was pacing about, obviously talking on her mobile.

She laughed. Then she said, "No problem, Hugo. Talk soon."

Hugo. Of course, she could know someone else by that name.

He listened for a moment and then cleared his voice.

Avalyn stepped into the passage. "Oh, hello, Simon! How are you?"

"Good morning." Simon noticed that she kept her face controlled with a smile that didn't quite reach her eyes. Her voice was light and airy. Apparently, she had no intention of castigating him for his sister's assertion that she no longer needed help. He said, "Things going well, are they?"

"Well, I am happy to say, I am rather busy! In fact, I have a client due any moment, so our visit may be a little short. What brings you to the village?"

No forthcoming explanation about the caller named Hugo. Despite not wanting to be bothered, Simon was.

"Uh, I was just stopping at the council office, to make sure the bench was acceptable."

"And surely they were delighted?"

"Yes, actually, I think they were."

"That's wonderful, Simon. And what's your next project then?"

His mind went blank. Behind him, the door opened. He turned. "Good morning, Mr. Wilkinson. I was just leaving." Simon recalled Mr. Wilkinson and old Doctor Clewley had a disagreement, years ago, about who was going to buy a certain tract of land down by the river. The whole village got involved, and in the end, the farmer refused to sell to either of them. He figured Wilkinson was pleased to see a new health professional for his diabetes, if only because word may get back to Clewely about it.

With a quick goodbye, Simon was out of the door.

Walking the length of the village, Simon had a think about what he had heard at Avalyn's office. After a few minutes, he moved on to a bit of a self-talk to stir up his confidence, and then went to see Julius Vandersteen.

In his shop, Vandersteen sold mostly antiques, but Simon knew that he liked to keep rotating his merchandise and he did a vigourous business online as well. The greying gentleman had classical music tinkling from some unseen speaker, and he greeted Simon warmly. "Ah, Simon Whiston. I've heard that you finished a lovely bench for the green. Well done, Simon. We older folks have long wanted somewhere to rest our bones when we're walking about. Would you like a cup of tea?"

They spoke for a while about people they knew and what lovely autumn weather they were having. Simon knew that Mr. Vandersteen was never in a hurry, and appreciated a cuppa and a chat with those who came in his shop.

"I don't suppose you may be open to a business proposition, Mr. Vandersteen?"

"Simon, you know how much I admire your work. Whatever you want to build, son, I will sell for you."

Simon was touched by the old man's generosity, and his confidence in Simon's ability. There was no doubt that he had heard of Simon's business being lost, along with his health and his marriage. Mr. Vandersteen obviously believed in grace and moving forward. Plus, Simon reasoned, he really had nothing to loose, and perhaps a lot of money to be made.

"Of course, the pricing would be at your discretion, Mr. Vandersteen. And naturally, when you get paid, I get paid. Strictly on a commission basis."

"How can I refuse, Simon? I consider myself fortunate to be the first broker of your new business. At least, I hope I hold that honour?"

Simon laughed. "Absolutely, I haven't spoken to anyone but you. For now, you'll be the sole representative of my work."

They drank some more tea, and made further plans. Mr. Vandersteen told Simon that younger customers were frustrated with the low-quality offerings in entertainment units that didn't work with their 32-inch televisions, and assorted smaller technology. Older customers requested something different to the vast offerings of large, modern, square pieces for every room of the house, without needing to resort to buying antiques, which some people didn't want.

He told Simon of one woman from Maidstone who came in his antiques shop and called it "old and smelly."

"They seem to be looking for something else besides Scandinavian or shabby," he told Simon. In short, they seemed to be looking for Whiston's furniture range—well-made but not out of date, stylish without being stuffy.

It was exciting to imagine the possibilities, and to know there was still a strong market, two years on, for what he excelled in crafting. People weren't always content to bring home flat pack, Vandersteen had said. As Simon drove back to the farmhouse, his mind was buzzing with ideas of what he could make first, where he would source the materials, and when he would be able to deliver his first piece to Julius. It would take a little time to save money from his paychecks for the wood, but he was sure that Lorna would allow him to hold a little back. He daydreamed about branding a finished piece of furniture with his old logo.

The logo that had introduced him to Dominique.

He wondered how his ex-wife was doing. Perhaps she had realised she had truly loved him, despite whether his bank account was full or not. Maybe, now that he was feeling better, Dominique would want to hear from him. She wouldn't be upset by any more hospital visits. Now that he was eating, sleeping, and working like a normal human being, it seemed that his health had been sorted out, naturally. He liked the idea of calling her, telling her that he was back in business again. He would wait until his first piece sold, and perhaps take a chance and get in touch with her. He wondered if she still lived in their old home. It was a desirable neighbourhood, and not many of those rambling old homes in Chelsea came on the market very often, so perhaps there was an off chance that Hugo would know if she'd sold up.

Hugo. Simon had been so absorbed in his enthusiasm for carpentry that he'd quite forgotten about Avalyn. He could hardly be annoyed with Avalyn for chatting to Hugo on the phone when he was thinking about how he could impress his ex-wife. Especially since his ex-wife had had another man. What was he thinking? If he were honest, it was his pride that wanted to show Dominique that he'd survived; he had no real love left for her.

He found his sister on the sofa, in the same sort of dour mood as when he'd gone.

"Please, Simon, take Peony outside for a bit. She's doing my head in. It just isn't fair to a three year old to confine her to the lounge and kitchen. She's been such a good girl, really, only a bit too much energy. And she may have to go to the loo by now."

Simon took Peony to the bathroom, and then outdoors. She loved to ride her bike, with stabilisers to keep her upright, on the smoothest, worn part of the drive. Peony finally exhausted her energy, as evidenced by less pedalling and more talking. Her cheeks had grown rosy when Simon told her it was time to go back into the house.

As Peony walked through the door, a delivery van pulled up. Simon signed for the package, and took the stiff envelope to his sister. Simon pulled off Peony's jacket and gave her a drink of water.

"What's this?" Lorna said, opening the envelope.

"I don't know, I didn't look at it."

"Oh, my word, it's from Hugo. It looks so official."

"Untle Simon, here are my sho-durs."

"That's lovely, Peony. Where are your toes?"

She giggled and pointed to her feet.

"Well done!"

"It's a cheque, Simon."

He came to his knees by the sofa, to study the enclosed letter with his sister. It hadn't been so very long ago that he wouldn't have been able to go down on the floor, or stand back up, and he reflected for a moment at his improved health.

"I don't understand." Lorna handed the letter to Simon.

Simon scanned the document. "He's basically stating that you were working for him at the time of your accident, and therefore he's providing an incapacity benefit. It suggests that Hugo Harrop is the owner of the firm, and the firm is the owner of Miss Harrop's property."

"I am stunned. There's nearly four month's wages here, based on what I'd earn at the castle. And I am only half finished with the project. He must know after my discussion with his secretary that I wasn't meant to be finished, yet."

"I think, sister, that Hugo Harrop is quite taken with you."

"And to think of how rude and childish I was about his gorgeous lunch."

"Mmm."

"But Simon, I still don't trust him."

"It wouldn't be too difficult to figure that you'd need some cash flow during your recovery, so I am certain he wanted to pay you for the work you'd already done before the accident. What possible gain would he receive from this kindness, except that you think well of him?"

She stared at her brother with a blank expression.

"You're being paranoid, Lorna. Okay, I'll play the devil's advocate. Suppose he is trying to buy affection. Do you think that he couldn't find any women in London to seduce with his money?"

"Well, that's just it. Why me?"

"As your brother, I take offense to that statement. Why not you?" He kissed Lorna on the forehead and went to his father's old desk to make some drawings. As he walked away, Simon added, "Harrop's a good guy. You're simply not used to anyone who's considerate and respectable, present company notwithstanding."

Simon sat at his father's old wooden desk, opened a side drawer, and retrieved a pen and paper. His thoughts lingered on the conversation he'd overheard at Avalyn's office. He hoped that his sister was the only woman to whom Hugo was showing a particular fondness.

Simon wandered around the workshop, pleased that every trace of his father's garage business was gone, with the exception of the motorcycle that he and Finley were restoring. He allowed his imagination to create the perfect workshop. There were three garage doors in the shop. In front of the first, by the walk-in door, he planned to store wood. In the centre, he'd have his workspace, in front of the workbench that now held his tools. There would be room for basic equipment, plenty of power for cords, and it was beneath one of the large windows so the lighting was good. The third garage door would stand in front of temporary storage; there he'd stand up pieces that were being stained, or were finished and awaited delivery. The office adjacent to the garage still held some old files, but he could easily have a clear out. There was a large desk, and several chairs, a bookshelf full of old car manuals that he would dispose of, and the old metal file cabinet. The office was a good size, perfect for a computer, the order board system that he preferred, and other business necessities. It was daunting and thrilling to imagine getting back into business. He knew that Julius Vandersteen didn't suffer fools: he wouldn't have agreed to take on merchandise from Simon if there was no potential of an easy sale and good profit. Simon felt badly about asking his sister for help, but his new venture required it. The money from Hugo was a stroke of luck, and the timing was perfect. He knew that he was a good businessman, and he had a solid plan. There was even a contingency if he couldn't complete the work on the furniture. He had spoken with two men he'd worked with when he was an apprentice. They agreed to be part of his back-up plan—for a healthy cut of the money, but nonetheless, he would have help to finish should he require it.

That evening, he mentally reviewed his plans over and again, and was rather quiet at the dinner table. Lorna seemed preoccupied as well, and Simon feared that she had already decided what to do with the money sent to her from Hugo.

As night fell, Lorna organised Finley for the following day of school. Peony was already fast asleep. Simon helped his sister downstairs and began preparing their tea. They had an unspoken agreement to talk at the kitchen table. With his plan clear in his mind and the children tucked up in bed, Simon was speaking quickly, and began to pace the kitchen. "I just need a bit of capital. Not much, because I kept all of my tools and I can get by without other equipment right now, but I need to purchase the wood. I want to produce four different pieces, and see what sort of response people have. Sort of a market test. Then I am not sure if I can do French polishing by hand anymore, to finish the furniture properly. I may need to hire someone on."

Lorna knew her brother was brilliant when it came to planning his projects, and she was sure he'd thought of everything. Simon had been far more successful, with a good business sense, than anyone else in their family. "Alright, then."

Simon grinned. "I'll make a tidy profit for the household purse, I assure you."

"Are you quite sure? Or will it be, 'But Lorna, if you'd only feed the children fresh insects for another week, and let me buy more wood, then I could make another bookshelf.'"

He resisted the urge to tickle her. "Your bum leg is saving you right now. I'd have you screaming for mercy, you know."

Instinctively, she put her hands up in defense, and giggled from the memory of his previous abuse. "We'll be off to the bank, first thing in the morning. You can take the money you need to buy wood and whatever else."

"Cheers, Sis. And tomorrow, you're to stop suspecting Hugo and Avalyn of being conspirators of some kind, yes?"

"If that means you're asking if can she come back, the answer is no."

"Lorna, why are you being so stubborn? Everything was wonderful. Then you hear a piece of old news, and you go off people entirely. It's ridiculous."

"I don't know. I feel there's something suspicious in their history."

He decided not to muddy the water further by telling his sister that he'd walked into the clinic as Avalyn was finishing a call with someone called Hugo. "Not too suspicious, however, to cash Hugo's cheque."

"Right," Lorna replied. They smiled. "Honestly, Simon, I am still interested in Hugo, but that doesn't mean I want to contend with his ex-girlfriend flitting around my kitchen. It's not as though she doesn't live a stone's throw away. I am hardly keeping you from her."

"I suppose you're right. It's me who's let her down." He'd been so consumed with this plans for getting back into business again, he'd hardly given her a thought all day.

"I haven't seen her car at the usual time. Perhaps she's rather busy at the clinic, now?"

"Probably," Simon agreed. He was glad that Lorna had accepted Avalyn's competency as a nutritional therapist. "It was only a matter of time before people would warm to her. Anyway, the truth is, I have an idea about all of the domestic bit, as well."

Simon told his sister about Favor, the refugee from his driving service that wanted to work with children. "The last time I saw her, she said that she was told the reason she wasn't brought on is because she had no references. We could give her a start, and she could help you while I am in the workshop. Then I wouldn't be concerned about you or the children, and I could put together furniture for Julius Vandersteen to sell as soon as possible. Promise me you'll think about it."

"I don't have to think about it. The poor girl, completely alone in the world. Of course she can come. But what am I to do with her? Surely you're not going to drive her back and forth to the other side of Maidstone twice a day, and we're already rather tightly packed, aren't we?"

"It's probably not much of a kindness, but she could take my little room and I could sleep on the sofa," Simon said, thumbing in the direction of the sitting room. "Speaking of, it occurs to me to wonder why our dear old dad had a pair of desks. There's another out in the workshop office, so I think we ought to move this desk out of the box room and sell it off."

Lorna agreed, and said that she and the children always sat at the kitchen table.

Simon had figured on how they could get Favor where she needed to be. "Her weekly appointment is the day I work, so naturally I could take her back to the city with me, and she could check in at her flat as well. She's been through such hell, that, honestly, it probably still seems lovely for her to be safe, sleep indoors, and have food. I don't want to take advantage of her, but whatever little bit we could pay her is more than the nothing she's making now. If our giving her a reference helps her get a real job, then we've done her a good turn. I can't think she would stand to lose any benefits for this temporary position, since it would only be a short time until your leg's improved. She just needs a start; something on an otherwise blank CV."

"Well, if she says no to coming for a few weeks to help us out, I would still like to invite her to visit. I want to meet her, and it would be a treat for the children to talk to an African lady a little."

"A treat or a trauma. Joking, of course; she would be sensitive to their age and obviously she understands their life here in England."

"While we're being so enterprising, I want to do something new and exciting as well."

"Really, what's that?"

She smiled and laced her fingers together, stretched her hands in front of her as though pushing away opposition. "I've always dreamt of having my own stall."

Simon laughed. "Like a mare?"

"No, you idiot. At the village fete. When I dreamt of it before I wanted to win the pie contest, and go into business selling dozens of them and then have money to buy clothes. Naturally, this fantasy was before my darling little ducks came, because now I'd want to buy special birthday presents for Fin and Peony. And now I am off my feet, so I can't bake pies."

"Thank you for sharing."

"No, wait. You see I've thought of something else I could do besides bake."

"Which is most welcome, since you've never baked in your life —"

"And the stall fee isn't really that much, and my stall would be especially nice with my brother, the amazing furniture designer, doing it up for me."

"Don't lets drag me into it, until you tell me what you intend to do."

Her eyes sparkled. It occurred to Simon that perhaps this was one of the few things his sister had wanted to do–for herself–in a long time. Her adult life had comprised of cleaning up after others and taking care of her children. Not to mention getting her heart broken several times into the bargain.

"I want to knit things."

"Do you knit, Lorna?"

"No."

"All right, then. Am I off to the library tomorrow for a book?"

"No. I've been watching videos online. Can't be that difficult."

"Right. I'll get you signed up for a stall at the fete, then, and I'll buy wool for you when I am next in Maidstone, shall I?"

"You must be joking. I'll send an email to the fete committee. And I'll choose my wool when you take *me* to Maidstone this weekend. I don't want you coming home with balls of wool the color of oak, ash, and cherry wood."

"Fair enough."

It was frustrating to receive the wonderful cheque from Hugo, and not be able to express her gratitude. Lorna tried to ring Hugo on his mobile but was immediately sent to voice mail. Then she'd placed a call to Hugo's office, but was told that he was on business in Amsterdam for a few days. Not even the ever-efficient Margaret was available. Lorna wondered if she travelled with Hugo, or perhaps had taken time off because he was away.

The weather had changed ever so slightly, with a little snap of chill in the air. The skies were a brilliant cobalt blue, brightening her bedroom and lifting her mood. A small trip to the village this morning would be delightful. She'd been housebound for far too long. Perhaps after they had finished at the bank, Simon could be talked into a coffee at the charming café in Stonewyck, or some other frivolous indulgence. Tired of sweatpants, Lorna resorted to cutting the leg off an old pair of jeans to accommodate her orthopaedic boot. She pulled on one of her old favourites, a soft wool, pine-green sweater. Soon, she'd be knitting jumpers like this one.

Lorna made her way very slowly and cautiously down the farmhouse staircase. Simon was on the floor with Peony, talking to her about the sticker book she was working. They gathered the envelope from Hugo, and made their way to Simon's van.

They settled Peony in her car seat. The back of Simon's old delivery van was devoid of seats, so Lorna took a precarious seat on an upturned bucket behind Simon. "You'll be alright, love?"

"It's not far," Lorna replied. She began to have a re-think about taking a drive to Stonewyck, and arriving at the neighbouring village with the imprint of a bucket on her bum. Perhaps just stopping at Goodchild's to get Peony some sweeties would suffice as something to do besides the boring errand to the bank.

They arrived in Burleigh Cross. Simon parked at the modest provincial bank, located in one of the newer buildings in the village, behind the pub. They went inside to cash Hugo's cheque, and also an insurance settlement made on Lorna's car. She'd been looking at adverts online for another used car to buy, but the offerings were rather dismal. After Janelle, the bank teller, had deposited Lorna's unexpected income, Simon, Peony and Lorna made their way out of the building. As they opened the door, Mrs. Sweeney was coming in. Lorna bristled; Mrs. Sweeney was the wheezy little co-hort that followed Miss Harrop around, peering stupidly through her thick glasses and nodding her head when old Miss Harrop was verbally abusing some poor soul. All better thoughts of Miss Harrop vanished, as Lorna recalled memories of Mrs. Sweeney nodding at her while Miss Harrop had shouted Peony's guilt all over the village. Lorna felt as though she could smack old Mrs. Sweeney, too.

"Oh, oh, Miss Whiston," Mrs. Sweeney said, with a sniff. Her voice was shaky and lacked the volume of her friend. Simon, hearing the old woman speak to her sister, instantly picked up Peony and came to stand close to Lorna. "Did Miss Harrop ring you?"

Lorna was stunned by the question. And stunned too, wanting to know how you could be 'friends' with someone for fifty years and still refer to them by their surname. "Actually...yes, she did, some weeks ago."

"I thought as she may," mumbled Mrs. Sweeney, peering at Lorna through her thick glasses. "She's not right, mind you. Has a few old phone numbers in her handbag, and your mother's is one of 'em, see."

Lorna didn't comprehend Mrs. Sweeney at first. Then she remembered that it was the old land-line telephone that Miss Harrop's call had come through. Lorna exchanged a look with Simon, and said, "Oh, I see. And you say that Miss Harrop has been ill?"

"Oh yes. For a long time, but mind you, what could anyone do? It was probably best that she had that little infection, what when you found her. So as she could get help, see. Someone from the home phoned one afternoon. Miss Harrop was having a good day, then. She'd wanted me to know where she was living and asked them to ring me. And the nurse, she did."

"Yes. Right. Have you been to see Miss Harrop?"

"My Agnes, she took me to London for my niece's recital. Our Edy plays piano, you know. I had the address given me by the nurse. And that's when we was to visit Miss Harrop, but when she saw me, she didn't know me. After'n all these many years, she didn't know me."

Mrs. Sweeney pondered this fact and turned to walk away. Lorna wondered if perhaps Mrs. Sweeney wasn't altogether there, either, as she'd just drifted out of their conversation. Simon turned and Lorna followed him to the van.

They were putting Peony in the car seat when Lorna said, "Excellent."

"What?"

"Now I know that Hugo was telling the truth about Miss Harrop needing to live in a care home."

Returned from Amsterdam, Hugo rang the following afternoon.

"I could not believe it, when I received the money you sent,"

Lorna said, before hello. "It was wonderfully generous, Hugo. What possessed you?"

"We never agreed on a payment amount, but I'd always intended to match your fee with what the clear-away service wanted for their part, plus a little extra for pain and suffering. You wouldn't have been in that accident, had you not been working at my auntie's house."

"Not quite sure I deserve your generosity, but I did cash the cheque!"

Hugo laughed. "I should hope so."

"I felt badly about leaving your beautiful lunch a bit early. Truly, it was one of the loveliest things ever done for me. And thank you for the gifts, too."

"My pleasure. I hope the non-slippy socks helped you out."

"They did, mostly by making me laugh," Lorna said, remembering the moment she had opened his present in the middle of the night, after she'd tired of pouting. "Thank you, again, Hugo." She felt as though she must have some resolution, and so finally posed the question. "Hugo, can I ask you something rather personal?"

"Uh-oh."

She giggled. "Tell me about you and Avalyn."

"I wondered if that wasn't going to be a bit of a sticking point."

"Should it be?"

"No. But I imagined you might have been wondering about our history. It doesn't take long to explain. We went out a half-dozen times, maybe less. I love to eat out, loads of beef dinners and such. Avalyn loves to stay in and cook vegetables or something exceedingly wholesome and thus began our incompatibility. I moved to London because I wanted to escape the countryside. Avalyn said she wished to escape the city. I want to go to a game or the cinema. She would prefer a dusty museum. Our conversations were at adverse purposes, even more so than what I ordered for pudding. You see the pattern?"

Lorna was in stitches. "It's crystal. And she couldn't be more right for my brother, I assure you. They'll probably take up bird watching any day. So, how was Amsterdam?"

He told her. Endless meetings, too much coffee. He usually went twice a year, and was glad to have it off his diary for a while.

"I went somewhere infinitely more exciting," Lorna said, telling him about the wool shop. He expressed interest and asked her the date of the autumn fete, so that he could drop by before it closed up.

"Yes, you really ought to come. It's your sponsorship that is causing this starving artist to be able to sell her wares."

They made plans for another date. He wanted to bring her to Maidstone for dinner. "I'd take you to a film, but I am not sure your leg is ready for that, especially since we'd be spending a bit of time driving." Lorna realised he'd given it all some thought and she felt flattered.

"Until then, love."

"Alright, Hugo. Looking forward. Goodnight."

Chapter Seventeen

IT WAS DIFFICULT to pull himself away from constructing his first piece of furniture for Julius Vandersteen, but Simon had to keep working his job as a van driver for the county– at least for the present. He saw Favor as expected, and he hoped to help her take another step from being a refugee to an employed citizen. She boarded the van with a cheerful smile and sat immediately behind him, clutching some sort of papers that she would give to the job and benefits centre counsellors. Favor's espresso-coloured skin was gleaming with a bit of misty rain. Given the slight chill in the air, she'd donned a truly hideous jumper with a carrot-nosed snowman on the front, and a riot of large round snowflake-circles on a bright blue background. Simon thought Favor looked a bit less horrid than most people would have; the yarn pom-pom of the snowman's hat bobbing about picked up the incredible white of her smiling teeth.

"Hello Favor," Simon said, hitting a button for the transport van door to close. "I've got an idea for you to consider."

"Oh, dat sounds good," Favor said, laughter ringing out in the otherwise empty vehicle.

Simon told her of his sister's need for a bit of help with the children and the house for a few weeks. He stressed that the duties would be light, and although the pay was modest, she could add temporary employment to her CV. She was delighted and accepted the position immediately. "I will have sumthing to say to de lady at de job centre today!" she said. "And if you can wait for me to pick a suet case, I will be ready in tree minutes to drive to your farm home wit you at de end of to-day." Simon said those were his thoughts exactly, and during his lunch break he rang Lorna to tell her that Favor would be joining their household for a couple of weeks, or until Lorna was able to get back on her feet, most literally.

That evening, Finley and Peony were immediately drawn to Favor and her soft-spoken, interesting accent. They asked her many questions, most of which had to do with safari animals. They seemed to understand her without difficulty.

Peony introduced Favor to Gemma Giraffe.

Favor told her lovely stories about giraffes she'd seen on her travels and she shared Peony's fascination for their spots, long legs, and sumptuous eyelashes. The young African woman enchanted the children, and Favor seemed equally fond of her charges. Simon had moved his father's old desk from the box room at the back of the sitting room, and Lorna had done her best to cheer up the room a bit with a house plant, rug, a small basket of sweets, and a stack of recent magazines beside the storabed.

The next morning, Lorna woke to the sound of someone in the kitchen. Minutes later the wonderful smell of breakfast wafted up the stairs. She couldn't fathom why Avalyn would return, uninvited.

Lorna managed to get herself to the loo, but was impatient for Simon's help on the stairs, which seemed more of a challenge early in the morning since her fall and subsequent bruising. She stood leaning against the wall, waiting for him and trying to peer into the kitchen from her elevated perch. Favor appeared at the bottom of the steps, smiling and climbing towards her.

"I wheel heep you down," she said, expertly holding Lorna beneath the elbow. Favor was a tall, strong girl, and as good as Simon at helping her.

"You're cooking?"

"I am a good cook!" Favor said. Lorna instinctively knew that Favor wasn't prideful, but rather took pride in doing things well. She was simply stating a fact. They toddled down the steps together and the enticing breakfast smells engulfed her.

"Lovely," Lorna whispered. Indeed, the breakfast table was set and ready. Favor had made some sort of egg pie, stuffed with meat and vegetables, which sat steaming on the cooktop. There were stacks of buttered toast, sliced on the diagonal, with a jar of marmalade open and standing at the ready with a knife alongside. The children were clean, dressed, and sat at the table. They were smiling and looked like an ideal family on a television advertisement.

"Gemma says its delishshush, Mummy!"

"I am so impressed, Favor. Where is Simon?"

"He is at work, in dat big building. He is happy with his wood, and I reckon he will come to the house when he is hungry."

Lorna laughed. "You're very perceptive."

A prayer was said, and they enjoyed Favor's outstanding cooking. Lorna was struck by the thought that, after being a single mom for so many years, here was the second woman in the space of a month to be cooking and cleaning for her. She thought it rather unbelievable, especially given the fact that her previously estranged brother had been the means for these women to come into their lives, to be so kind to her and her kids.

Finley left for school, and Lorna was reading to Peony when Simon came in for breakfast.

"You missed one of the best breakfasts I've ever eaten," Lorna said.

"Gemma said it was delishshush!" Peony added, again, using her new favourite word.

"It's a sort of breakfast casserole, and you can microwave yours."

"Alright. What's Favor doing now?"

"She's beavering away upstairs. I've no idea really, but she seems to have boundless energy, and I would imagine she's cleaning something that I've wanted to clean since I broke my leg. I tried to tell her we're not paying much and she doesn't have to lift a finger except to help me a bit and look after Peony a few minutes here and there, but there's no stopping her."

"I am not surprised," said Simon, loading his plate with food from the casserole dish pulled from the fridge. "She seems to enjoy work, and I think she's had quite enough of sitting in that grotty little flat with nothing to do for days on end."

"Well, lucky us."

His breakfast reheated, Simon said, "This *is* delicious, Peony," and forked more food into his mouth while scooting a chair back from the table with his foot.

"Better than Avalyn's cooking?"

"Lorna, leave it. I do miss her, you know."

"But hammering and sawing wood is a close second, I imagine."

"Hideous wench. You're just jealous I can walk to the garage."

"You know, I believe there's some truth in that."

At the clinic, the week was the most fruitful that Avalyn had had in Burleigh Cross. One of her patient's revealed the reason for some of her new found success.

"It was Mrs. Jones who sent me, and I know she's sent along a few others," said one of Avalyn's new patients, a woman whose family had been farming outside the village for five generations. "She's the best mid-wife in the county, is Mrs. Jones, and she said she knows of three cases where the ladies who saw someone about nutrition were able to come off their medicine. So, that's why I am here. I want to have a baby, you see, and the doctors said I couldn't have one, not as big as I am. They insist that's part of the problem, even though I am not sure; my sisters are my size, and they've each got three kiddies. But they did have problems with sugar and blood pressure, which is no good. I said to my Gerald, why not give it a go? If you tell me what to do, I'll do it."

Avalyn found Mrs. Jones, the mid-wife, in a directory and rang her up. She thanked her for sending patients her way. Avalyn posted business cards to Mrs. Jones, should she want to send along anyone else. It was exciting to have a colleague in the community who appreciated her skills, and she hoped for opportunities to refer pregnant women to Mrs. Jones when appropriate.

Avalyn decided that having a stall at the autumn fete would be an effective means to advertise her practice. The fact was, she despised self-promotion, and that was one of the reasons she was so delighted that Mrs. Jones had taken it upon herself to give her a boost. Yet, she needed to get the word out about what she could offer people in the village and surrounding communities. Since a fete was nothing without food, and she loved to be in the kitchen, it was fairly obvious what she ought to do.

And then again, not.

When it came to food, she had no idea who usually made what, and didn't want to step on the toes of some farmer's wife who always brought her prize-winning specialty. Since Lorna didn't seem very chummy at the moment, she had thought she may have a chat with her lovely friend, Emily Norcross, for a few ideas. Molly Myers, the friendly proprietress at Goodchild's and one of the sponsors of the fete, would probably provide some clues as well.

Avalyn asked both women, and concluded that although there was an abundance of pies, cakes, toffee apples, and one person hiring a machine to do candyfloss, no one in Burleigh Cross seemed to specialize in muffins or cupcakes. Avalyn had an idea of making "healthy" mini-muffins. Inspired and excited, she looked forward to reviewing her recipes. She would select the best, and offer them by the dozens from her stall at the fete.

She arrived back at the cottage that evening, and decided to walk Gus on the path that wound through the farm behind her home. He was elated, and his great tail pumped to and fro while he shuffled from one enthralling scent to another.

Walking alone with her dog, Avalyn longed for Simon's company. It had been a week since he had stood in her office. As soon as she'd seen him, anger gave way to a rising hope in her heart. She had tried to read his eyes, but learned nothing of his feelings. Mr. Wilkinson had cut their meeting short. Avalyn remembered mentally pleading with Simon as he turned to leave. *Ask me to lunch. Ask me to dinner. Ask me if I love you, Simon, because I do.*

As the sun set over the fields, she and Gus turned towards home.

The orangey sky did nothing to warm the air, and she shivered. These days, having to deal with coats, keys, and getting the shopping done were things that she accomplished rather mindlessly. Avalyn took stock of her existence. The days wore on as she carried on with her work at the clinic. In the evenings, she often found herself in the middle of the sitting room, or standing at the kitchen sink, unsure what errand had brought her there, consumed by scenarios of what had transpired between she and Simon. Perhaps Simon was ill again, and trying to protect her from his deteriorating condition? Or maybe Lorna had some unknown crisis that had quite taken over his spare time– something to do with the children? Most certainly, he'd come to the conclusion that he had no feelings for her. That being too painful to consider, she'd push it aside.

She forced herself to think of the relationship in logical terms, to begin again at the beginning, to patiently sort through each conversation, look, and touch, to endeavor what was meant by his silence. She kept it all at arm's length, because if she dwelled on certain memories, she'd start sobbing again.

"Don't worry, baby, you'll never be on your own again." Those were his words, the ones she guarded her heart against; hearing his voice, remembering the tenderness in his eyes, inevitably ended in tears.

Lorna was delighted with the selection at the wool shop in Maidstone. Simon helped her hobble along the rows of gorgeously coloured wool, arranged a chair for her to sit upon while she carefully reviewed the pattern books, and helped her select her first knitting needles based on the list she'd made while researching on the Internet. Lorna had a particular yen for the fuzzy, pastel coloured yarns. "What do you think of the mint and lavender, Simon?" she asked her brother.

"Are you planting a garden or knitting?"

"Ha. That brings up a good point: don't pretend you are without an opinion. Any man who can design furniture and work Mum's garden should have a thought."

This earned him a sideways glance from an attractive girl carrying a shopping basket.

"You're a clever Miss Marple, then. You decide," he said in an offhanded tone to preserve his dignity. The girl passed into another aisle of the shop. His sister waited, intent on receiving his reply. Like her mate, Emily, Simon always thought of something that she hadn't, so it was worth pressing him for his opinion.

"Alright. Will it matter much that you've got all those Easter sorts of colours? Isn't the fete meant to be celebrating autumn, and women might well be thinking of Christmas presents?"

Lorna's mouth dropped open in surprise. "Oh, you are good, aren't you? I hadn't thought of all that. It's warm and sunny today, but it won't be in two weeks, will it? Then all this clobber will look completely wrong."

She wanted to dump the lot, but felt badly that someone else would have to sort the mess.

"Go on, Lorna, it'll give them five minutes of tidying. Those women at the counter have been chatting since we came in. Not to mention, I am entertaining thoughts of actually leaving before they close up."

Seasonal colours selected, Lorna took her purchases to the counter. She'd written down a few names of yarns that she would come back for when she was ready, but she had little idea of how much she needed. Best to begin with a small investment.

She slept in the van on the way home, exhausted from her foray back into the world. Simon woke her when they pulled into the farmhouse drive.

"I am going to be a textile artist," she said, smiling.

"But I refuse to allow you to dress the children in horrid, handmade Christmas jumpers."

Lorna laughed. "Even if they match?"

"Especially then." He left his side of the van, and came to retrieve her from the passenger's side. She dropped gingerly onto the gravel and took a moment to achieve balance.

"Simon?"

"Hmm?"

"You haven't spoken to Avalyn, have you? Because I am feeling rather guilty about her. Just because I don't want her cooking and in and out of the house thrice a day doesn't mean you ought to feel like I am presenting some mandate or other. You know I wasn't serious for two seconds put together about throwing you out, don't you?"

"My wool buying flair has earned me a place in my sister's good graces. Lovely."

"What's going on with you two?"

"I've just been rather busy with wanting to work on furniture again."

Lorna let it rest. Her brother was near impossible to push where he did not want to go.

They collected her purchases and noticed some lovely cooking smells emanating from the house. Favor had been busy.

Chapter Eighteen

IN ONLY TWO days, Simon's coffee table, the first piece of furniture that Julius Vandersteen would sell for Simon through his shop, was quickly taking shape. Simon derived great pleasure both from working uninterrupted during the day, and also having his nephew help him for a while after returning from school. Finley led the way as he and his uncle Simon came in from the workshop. "Mum, I am helping Uncle Simon, and he says I am brilliant at measuring." Simon smiled and tousled his hair.

"He has you and our Dad to thank for a good head for maths," Lorna said to her brother. "That's lovely, sweetie. You'll have less time to watch TV tonight, though. No skipping homework if you're going to learn to be a master craftsman."

"I know."

Simon saw that Favor was busying herself stirring something on the stove. She turned and tipped her head at them, signalling the family to be seated at the table.

"I hope you will like tis food," Favor said, and the Whistons smiled at her. "Beans and vegetables are nutris-ious and a good value for de money." She ladled a stew into large bowls, and produced a plate loaded with homemade, whole-grain crackers worthy of Prince

Charles.

Simon tucked in. Dinner was a bit unusual, but the children seemed to be coping. For his own part, he rather liked the exotic flavours It was somehow spicy, without having much heat.

"Favor's African-inspired cuisine is quite tasty, doesn't everyone agree?" Finley and Lorna nodded their heads. Finley had quickly embraced eating all manner of garden produce after Avalyn began cooking for them, and he said he thought the spices were "quite good". Favor beamed at the boy and he blushed slightly. Lorna loved anything that someone else made, and had told Simon that she was glad to have a little help keeping her weight down.

Only Peony wasn't sure. She eyed the beans suspiciously.

Favor cleverly addressed the little girl's concern. "Giraffes especially like good African cooking. There is a hotel with very high windows. A giraffe will visit anyone who opens the window and feeds it good African cooking." Peony imagined a very tall and graceful Gemma coming to her bedroom window to be fed. She giggled, a buoyant sound reminiscent of her mother, and dipped her spoon into the stew for a little taste. Favor smiled.

It's good for Favor to be here, Simon thought, *and good for us.* All the same, he felt a stab of regret that Avalyn was no longer regularly in their home, and part of his day. But he realised that he was grappling with other issues, too. Thinking rationally, he trusted Hugo to be faithful to his sister. And how daft would it be for he and Avalyn to carry on, when Simon need only gaze out the window to see Avalyn's cottage? Not to mention, Hugo wasn't the type to enjoy idiotic games of deceit. Logically, Simon wanted to be gainfully employed before taking things any further with Avalyn. Until he was re-established in work life, he felt he couldn't offer her much.

Unfortunately, things didn't seem that straightforward. When he'd overheard Avalyn speaking to someone called Hugo, it brought back Dominique's betrayal. A bit like getting knifed in the gut. Had there been warning signs that his wife was having an affair? It didn't make sense not to trust Avalyn. Definitely a spot of difficulty, overhearing Avalyn's phone call with some bloke. His emotions were in a tangle, and he couldn't seem to sort them out.

Maybe it was the same for her. Had she doubted her feelings for him? Perhaps she'd heard something in the village. A tale from London, something about Simon that wasn't even true. Hadn't Lorna said Miss Harrop thought he was a drunk? He'd already told Avalyn the truth, which was raw enough. No one need embellish it. But people often felt the need.

After dinner, he helped Favor with the washing up, and then sat down for a chat with his sister. Although she wasn't asked or expected to do so, Favor scooped up Peony and took her upstairs for her bath.

Lorna said, "Hugo is taking me out this weekend. We're going to Maidstone for dinner."

Of course he is, Simon thought. Because of course he isn't interested in Avalyn. Simon imagined making enough money on his furniture sales and being able to treat Avalyn to an expensive meal. The thought was enough to make him want to return to the workshop to work a bit longer, but admittedly he was knackered. "Are you wearing sweatpants or your cut up old jeans?"

His sister frowned. "I hadn't thought of that. What's going to look right with this bum leg?"

"You've got a few days to think about it. Knowing Favor, she probably can sew up something for you. She seems to be able to do everything else."

"True. I am amazed at her grasp on things. She comes from such a different culture, but knows how to fit right in, doesn't she? And she's fabulous with the children. I am so happy that you met her on your route, Simon. She's been a Godsend."

"That's what you said about Avalyn."

"Oh, dear. You're pining."

"Go ahead and have a laugh, Lorna, but don't forget it wasn't too terribly long ago that you were quite upset about Hugo."

"True. But I am enjoying being happy at the moment. Despite staggering around, and taking physio, it's lovely to have just a tiny bit of extra cash and have a great guy paying me attention. Even the autumn fete is something I am really looking forward to. Don't begrudge me."

Simon smirked.

"What's that for? You know, you've been quite chipper about your woodworking, but it seems you've gone off your precious Avalyn. What's going on?"

"I haven't gone off her. Just fighting a few demons, you know?"

"Alright. But you do know that women don't like being put off, don't you? Have you forgotten your way across the road?"

Simon drew in a breath. He had no wish to explain. His sister would accuse him of being full of pride. Or tell him he was being silly, and reprimand him, saying something along the lines of how he was so busy playing a knight that he'd lose the maiden. Despite her flippant comments, Lorna would understand his need to be his own man, before taking things any further with Avalyn. And how you can't move forward if you're looking backward. Nonetheless, she wouldn't come to it immediately. And he wasn't in the mood for guff. So he said, "I just wish I knew a bit more about our *friends.*"

"Well, I asked. He told me everything. He said they were polar opposites. They only went out a short while and he made it sound as though they couldn't agree on anything. As he talked, and having gotten to know *her* recently, I could imagine them together, and quite honestly, it made me laugh. What is it, Simon? You don't look relieved."

Abandoning common sense, he snapped at his sister. "If they were such a mash-up, then why has he rung up her office?"

Lorna was dismayed. "Are you sure?"

"Not entirely. But how many 'Hugo's' do you know?"

Chapter Nineteen

"OH, NO! SOD it." Lorna threw her knitting needles on the floor, the various sized knots she'd created were at once tightening and unraveling. She didn't care that the last three hours worth of work and frustration were unlooping themselves onto the rug. She was beyond concern that Peony, laughing and giggling, was picking up the lambs wool mass and pulling the funny sticks from the loops of aubergine-coloured wool.

She'd had *enough*. She wasn't a knitter.

Favor came running from the back of the house, leaving whatever efficient task she had been doing. She said nothing. Just waited with a blank face for Lorna to explain her outburst.

"I know I am a reasonably intelligent person. Here, you see, Favor, are simple, step-by-step instructions. I've watched the videos, the women on them showing how Peony ought to be able to do this. It isn't sodding brain surgery, is it? No. Meaning, if a reasonably intelligent person follows the simple instructions, she should end up with a lovely scarf for her craft stall at the village fete. But I *cannot knit!*"

Still, Favor was silent.

Here, standing in her house, was a woman who had overcome

adversity such as Lorna had ever known. Favor was the only person from her entire family who'd even survived. Lorna's crisis? She couldn't purl stitch.

"I am sorry, Favor. If this is my most challenging circumstance I am living a charmed life."

"I dink, Miz Lorna, we can make someting better, okay?"

"Alright. What do you have in mind?" She could imagine what was coming. Lorna tried to figure out what she would say to Favor. She would tell her the truth. "Sorry, love, but tribal baskets just won't move at the village fete. You understand." But would Favor understand?

"I will have a sample to show soon." Favor smiled.

When Favor smiled, the world lit up. Lorna could see all of the sunshine of Africa in her brown face and huge white teeth, and it cheered her immensely. She smiled back, wishing she could "beam" like that, but she knew that she simply looked like an English woman, grinning inanely. So. She couldn't knit. Or light up the room with a thousand watt smile, like Favor's rendition of Julia Roberts. It wasn't the end of the world. With Peony down for a nap, Lorna decided it was time to fold clothes while she watched a show. She would mentally check out until tea. As soon as she stuffed all of the knitting debris into a bag, and pushed it beneath the sofa, where she couldn't see it.

At lunch the following day, Lorna listened as Simon talked of the English sycamore, ebony, and applewood he'd chosen for his first piece of furniture for Julius Vandersteen. Excitement thrummed in his voice, and his gestures were decisive. He was in his element, being back to work, creating and building something. After working with the wood he'd perfected his original design, and had shown her the new details he had sketched. Even to her untrained eye, Lorna could see the piece was very sophisticated. It was classic coffee table, with graceful lines and lighter coloured, inlay border around its rectangular edge, a detail that probably wasn't seen in most furniture galleries these days. Simon was in the workshop from the early hours of the morning, coming in tired and pleased with himself after tea. With

Favor in the house, Lorna knew that Simon was free of concern of her tipping herself down the stairs or some other disaster.

Lorna also knew that Favor had been out to the workshop with Simon on two occasions, and suspected that it wasn't because Favor wanted to witness the progress of the coffee table. She knew it must have something to do with the craft project that Favor was working on, but Lorna didn't care to be curious. An entirely new feeling for her, perhaps, but at the moment she was consumed with finding something to wear on her date with Hugo. Her failed fete stall was as much extravagance as she allowed herself, so she wouldn't be taking herself shopping. The pair of older, sliced wide-legged jeans remained the best choice for covering her air boot, so she set her mind to pairing something with them. She'd teetered precariously up the highest run of narrow stairs, heavily supported by Favor, for a rummage through her mother's attic storage. There, from a full garment bag that was hanging on a rail, Lorna found a beautiful silk blouse. The soft periwinkle color looked lovely with her hair. It wanted airing out, but the blouse was in good nick and very romantic, perfect for a special date with Hugo, so long as they didn't go anywhere too smart for denim. Rummaging through a large box, Lorna discovered a vintage necklace that was sparkly, and it looked lovely with the blouse.

Lorna didn't usually do sparkly, but then she didn't usually dress up. Her first bloke, Finley's dad, hadn't taken her anywhere except the races, where sticky things ended up on the bottom of one's shoes. And with Peony's father, it was much the same. Rowan O'Riordan's tastes reached no further than the pub or perhaps taking in a music festival once a summer. Next to having her children, going out on the town with Hugo Harrop would be the highlight of her young life, especially now she knew she couldn't knit.

Lorna discovered a love of Mediterranean food. "You're not taking me to one of those chi-chi places with tiny little plops of food on a plate, are you Hugo?" she had asked him, giggling.

"Something along those lines, my country girl. However, I assure you, you're going to be angry with me that I haven't brought you here, sooner."

"Is that so?"

"Tis."

The hostess seated them in a pair of richly upholstered club chairs in a pattern of deep mulberry and warm grey, with a small, intimate table in between. The restaurant struck the perfect balance between comfort with a sense of privacy; a tastefully swank atmosphere with mouthwatering smells drifting from the kitchen. Lorna gave Hugo free reign to choose, and he ordered a selection of four small plates. When the waiter served them. Lorna giggled again, and said, "Oh, please. They're appetisers."

"Just eat." Hugo said, serving her various bits of this and that.

"Mmm, this is amazing," Lorna said. "What is it?"

"You won't like it if I tell you."

"No, really, Hugo."

"You're eating fried goat cheese coated with panko and lavender infused honey."

"Yes, of course, darling. I was just about to guess," Lorna said, taking a long sip of red sangria.

"This one is fattoush, which is a sort of salad that you'll have to try; I am sure I don't really know what it is. Bits of chicken in a rather Frenchy sort of sauce with celery, here. And my favourite, braised short rib of beef with pasta and freshly grated horseradish."

They ordered another round of the short ribs, and finished with shared pudding, a blackberry custard tart and chocolate cheesecake.

"Hugo, this has been really fabulous. Thank you," Lorna said. Hugo leaned in and stole a kiss. Lorna laughed and took the last bit of cheesecake.

Lorna had woken, and was contentedly tucked up in bed thinking about her evening with Hugo, when Favor knocked on her door. She came in wearing one of her dazzling smiles, and Lorna immediately noticed that she also wore a stunning necklace.

"Favor, where did you get that? It's beautiful." The deep blue necklace was made of many strands, with a fat knot on one side, accented with a piece of silver.

"Your magazines."

"What?"

"I med the beads from de magazine pages. Then strung them together. The paint was in the garage, from Finley's school project."

Lorna recognized the shade of blue from a banner Finley made last year.

"It is very shy-nee because of acrylic Mister Simon sprayed on top. No water ruin, and long lasting. What do you dink for your stall?"

Lorna had sat up in bed, saucer-eyed. "But I can't even knit."

Favor laughed, a big guffaw to go with her grand grin. She waved Lorna's concern away with a swipe of her hand in the air. "I promise you can do dis!"

Lorna found that she could. Favor had rolled strips of paper from Lorna's magazines around a duck bill shaped hair clip that she'd found in the bathroom cabinet, securing the paper ends with a bit of Finley's glue from his school supplies. A few moments of drying, and the "bead" could be slipped off the hair clip. The hair clip created an open centre in the paper, so the paper bead could be strung. Favor explained how to quickly paint the paper bead with the desired color, and finish with a protective spray of acrylic. Favor had strung her beads onto a hair ribbon that she'd borrowed from Peony's dressing up box, and tied it behind her neck. She thought a proper necklace thread would work better, but the ribbon came to hand.

"How did you think of this?"

"No, not me," Favor had said, wagging her finger back and forth to dispel any undue credit. "I met a woman from Gulu, in Uganda. She make dem, saying dey are paper pearls."

Lorna's mind was lively with possibilities. "Did it take you the last three days, though, to make one necklace?"

"Oh no, no!" Again the smile that made Lorna laugh, even though nothing was funny. Favor had a way of infusing joy into everyday situations, making others laugh along with her for no particular reason.

"I have stack of beads made, to show you different. Some short and round bead, some long as the end of your finger. Some beads, dey are fat, others skinny. All kinds, for different necklace, earring, and bracelet."

"The silver charm is beautiful; where did you get that?"

Another great laugh. "I don't know what dis is," Favor said, picking up the silver ornament of the necklace she wore, "But it was on Mr. Simon's workshop floor! It hooked right on des beads, and he said I could use it to show to you."

And so Lorna's foray into crafting jewellery from paper began. Knitting items were returned. Pots of various paints purchased, as well as glue, memory wire, acrylic, suede laces, and metal clasps. Lorna remembered the loads of magazines and newspapers left in tidy stacks at Miss Harrop's house; the service that Hugo hired explained that recycling of that kind was best done locally, and some of the magazines may be worth money. Lorna gained Hugo's permission to use whatever paper she and Favor needed for supplies. Wouldn't Miss Harrop have been surprised, Lorna thought.

Chapter Twenty

THE DAY OF the autumn fete was dismal. Rain poured, pelting against the tents, dampening spirits. Instead of riding the newly restored motorcycle, Simon loaded it into the van to bring it to the automobile show. Disappointment sapped Finley's energy, leaving him too depleted to whinge about the weather, and so carried himself off to find his friends. Some of the stalls remained unoccupied, rain dripping from the edges of the tents and splashing into puddles where the grass had worn away. A certain number of villagers made other plans for the day. Those with stalls dashed between the dry places under the eves of buildings or vehicles, and consoled each other with weather reports that the day was meant to improve.

The weather reports proved correct. Mid-morning brought a warming sunshine. The soaked lawn and colourful trees came alive in the brightening skies, and brought the fragrance of autumn. Dogs barked and children laughed as they played together. The car park slowly began to fill, as did the stalls. A band arrived and began to play.

Within an hour, the fete pulsed with energy.

Avalyn had arrived early to set up her stall, marching muffins on paper plates wrapped with cling film across the table, with a stack of recipes, and a basket of brochures outlining her available nutrition counselling. She'd seen Simon at a distance, helping his sister to set up a stall. Then he seemed to be making his way towards the automobiles with Finley in tow. She couldn't imagine why he couldn't take a moment to say hello, to wish her luck with her stall, as any friendly person ought to do. Of course, she told herself, she couldn't leave her stall to say hello to he and Lorna. Not to mention, she certainly didn't see the point in greeting people who had set her aside. Even so, she couldn't help snatching glances across the lawn at Simon's retreating backside. There was no trace of weakness, no hitch in his walk. He'd gained some weight and looked strong. He looked fit. *Really fit.*

Avalyn's insides tickled with cold self-pity. Perhaps he had met someone else. Each week, Simon's work took him to Maidstone. Maybe he'd met a woman from the office that dispatched him, or at a place where he stopped for lunch. She imagined him seated alone at some pub, having struck up a conversation with someone else who was eating alone. She had to smile as she suddenly recognised the scenario. That's how she'd met Hugo.

Lorna was staggered at the response to the jewellery that she and Favor had made. "The beads are made of paper," she insisted, but the doubtful looks she received didn't stop women from buying necklaces, bracelets, earrings, and one of the several dozen rings that Favor had surprised her with at the last moment.

Growing tired of leaning on sticks, Lorna took a seat against the back of the stall. Favor's selling abilities were a surprise. Unhindered by her accent, she smiled and spoke to each person who came to the stall, unless they approached Lorna first. Favor explained how the jewellery was made, and unabashedly pushed the product. "Here, put dis on, it weel be gorgeous on you!" she would say, and the woman in front of her joyfully obeyed, admiring the jewellery in their oval, tabletop-sized, mirror, another treasure that Lorna had found in the attic. Inevitably, Favor would pair the right pieces of jewellery with the right person and the sale was made, along with, "a gift for your mother, or sister, or friend, so happy tay will be." Though they'd brought almost a hundred pieces, merchandise was running out, thanks to Favor's quick, diligent work, and the fact that Lorna had had little else she could do during her final phase of healing. She had sat with Favor, making paper beads and jewellery most afternoons.

Favor said that she needed to use the ladies' and that she would bring them back something to eat. Lorna was rested and stepped forward just as a few more customers were coming towards the stall. She hoped she could sell the jewellery as well as Favor while she was gone, but she wasn't as comfortable with insisting that people try on the items. Favor did that so naturally, and Lorna could see that once a lady had on something pretty with a low price tag, it was a challenge for her to leave it behind. Not to mention the discounts that Favor had drawn on a card and propped up beside the mirror, for earning a free pair of coordinating earrings with the purchase of a necklace and bracelet.

"You may want to try it on, the bracelets are rather lightweight," Lorna bravely suggested to Molly Myers, her longtime acquaintance from the village. Lorna supposed that the owner of Goodchild's shop wouldn't be too put off by a bit of salesmanship. "I imagine you could wear one at the shop all day without it making you batty. They're quieter than other sorts of beads, too." Molly agreed and bought the bracelet. Lorna felt good about her sale, although two other women drifted away from her in the process. But perhaps they were making an initial survey of the stalls and would come back. She typically did a bit of window-shopping herself. Then again, she thought, a single mum with two kids often didn't make it back round to buy anything for herself.

Lorna had a brief lapse in customers. She wondered how Emily was coping; she'd volunteered to help with the pet registry for the fete dog show. Her eyes scanned the fete, taking in the bright colours, looking across at other stalls and their wares, noting that the pies brought to raise money for the school were down to only three. She wondered if they were expecting more pies, and thought perhaps she may try sometime to bake one. Perhaps Favor knew how and could show her, although she wasn't sure if fruit pies were eaten in Africa.

She saw Avalyn at the farthest stall, talking to a rather obese woman who probably was glad to learn that Avalyn held secrets to weight loss. Avalyn handed the woman some papers and something that the woman immediately stuffed into her mouth.

Suddenly, Lorna saw *him*.

Rowan O'Riordan had already seen her. Sporting his pirate's grin, he was sauntering straight towards her, allowing no time for her to compose herself. Tears immediately sprang to her eyes. She suddenly saw so much of him in Peony that it made her heart ache in an instant for the family they could have been.

"Hello, my love."

"Rowan. I shouldn't have thought you'd be interested in coming all the way from London for our little fete."

"Oh, you're quite wrong." He leaned across the display board Simon had constructed, grinding bracelets beneath his elbows. He was too close. His sour breath smelled of beer. Lorna felt powerless to step away, afraid she might forget how to manoeuvre on her crutches and take a fall. His eyes lingered over her, and she felt her skin prickle. Was she feeling excitement, or fear? When it came to Rowan, it all became a muddle.

"I am rather fond of village diversions. *You* should know that."

The tears came unbidden. Lorna despised her emotions being so visible to him, but there was no help for it. She couldn't leave the stall, and she knew if she tried to hobble away, he would just follow her anyway. She longed for Simon to come, but she knew that he was busy elsewhere; she hadn't seen her brother since they arrived.

"What do you want?" Her voice came in a hoarse whisper. Her own voice was a surprise, and full of a once familiar, sharp heartache that she hadn't felt in a long time.

"You, of course." Rowan leaned in and was kissing her before she could think of what was happening. Then he said, "I've made some money, you see. And I've come back to get you."

"You mean you want to get back together? You want to be a father?"

His eyes betrayed him, floating back and forth as he tallied. He obviously hadn't really thought things through regarding the children. Lorna was insulted, realising that Rowan thought he could simply show up and expect her to fall into bed with him. It seemed to him the best course to use a bit of guilt manipulation. "I was always a good daddy, when I wanted to be. You know that."

"You would come back here after *years* and expect me to leave the life I've managed to build." Her strength was returning; it had simply been the shock of seeing him before, she knew that, now. Spitefully, she added, "You can't be seriously that *stupid*."

She levelled her eyes with his, and in the periphery over his shoulder she saw Favor approaching, and felt courage rise within her. Gesturing for him to step back and stop squashing the merchandise, she said, "You really ought to move along."

He grinned sarcastically and stayed rooted to the spot; he was always one determined to have the last word. "Oh, so your 'life' here is such a grand affair, is it? It seems to me that you're lower than I left you. Got your crippled brother living with you, I heard, and it looks like you can't walk now, either. Got the same disease, I reckon. You're quite right, my love, I could do better."

And with that, he slithered away. At least she hoped he'd gone. Or was he just going to make trouble elsewhere? The triumph Lorna had felt throughout the jewellery making with Favor, the encouragement she'd gained in her relationship with Hugo, the fact that her leg was healing and Simon was doing well, all seemed obliterated in a moment. She had thought things were going so well, but now she saw things for what they really were: hardly changed. She was still a single mum, and her history with Hugo was rather brief. Maybe he didn't even care about her as a temporary employer, but had paid her off to avoid potential legal issues. And who knew if he was seeing another woman in London? Perhaps even Avalyn, as her brother had said that she was speaking on the phone with someone called Hugo.

As much as it was lovely to have help, it galled her that she hadn't been able to work—just as she hadn't, for very different reasons, when Rowan left her. Although Hugo's cheque had eased things for the moment, her recent high spirits were foolishness. She would be back cleaning toilets at the Castle accommodations soon enough, and barely making ends meet. Her brother would probably leave. And the doctor had been very clear: she'd had a rather bad break, and the pain could stay on. Sometimes patients didn't return to normal for a year or more, the surgeon had said. And she had a physical job, with two kids to take care of.

So many black thoughts crossed her mind within moments of seeing Rowan that Lorna felt quite unable to cope. She turned slowly to face the tented rear of the stall, fighting against tears.

Favor came inside talking about their wonderful sales, and offering her food.

"Favor, I am really not up to this. I am going home, alright? We've sold most of the jewellery, so you probably will have to close up in an hour or two, at the most. Is that okay with you? I'll text my brother and let him know to look out for the children. I am sure that Emily won't mind to drive me."

She ignored the confused look on Favor's face and painfully shuffled away on her sticks.

"That's a fair lookin' bike you've got there," Rowan O'Riordan said. His statement was complimentary, but his eyes were full of menace. Rowan was joined by a stout, unsmiling man who looked in need of a bath. Their fingers ringed cups of beer.

Simon nodded. Deciding to be civil, he replied, "She's for sale, if you have any interest."

Rowan threw back his head and laughed. "I suppose that'd be right. I've done with your sister, so maybe I can take this off the farm, eh?"

"I think it's time you clear off, O'Riordan."

"Oh, are we having a 'good day', Simon? Feel strong enough to take me on, do you?"

"I do." And Simon did.

His fist made contact with O'Riordan's jaw, and sent him reeling backwards. The man caught his balance, but spilled his beer. His mate, tough looking but unwilling to be involved, stepped back, leaving the lads plenty of room.

Two of the men from the village, George Myers from Goodchild's shop, and Ernie the postman, came and stood beside

Simon.

"Alright, then, Whiston, I can see you've got your middle-aged outlaws here. No need to fuss. You say hello to my daughter for me, won't you? Maybe I'll drop by and visit her next time I am in the village."

Chapter Twenty-One

LORNA WAS SO engrossed looking at the clouds through the window above the sofa that she didn't notice the noise of a vehicle on the drive. Startled, she realised that someone was pounding on the door.

Easing herself up on her crutches, she felt a bit dizzy. She neglected to eat anything that Favor had brought back to the stall at lunchtime, and now it was hours later. She froze where she was, halfway across the room, and took a deep breath.

And then a thought occurred. What if Rowan was at the door? He hadn't been above hitting her, not to mention being insulting, when he'd been drinking. It was late afternoon, but that didn't mean he hadn't been over at the pub, nursing a grievance about the way she'd spoken to him earlier. She felt terror spread through her middle, and up through her neck, ending in a hot prickling sensation across her scalp.

"Lorna?" The caller was a familiar male voice. But it was Hugo.

Flooded with relief, she began a choppy progress towards the door. She finally opened it, and then began hopping to one side, allowing Hugo clearance to come in. Her breath was ragged. She hoped he'd assume it was from the effort of coming to the door.

"What're you doing here, love?" he said after laying his hands on her shoulders and kissing her. "Did you get tired after the big sell-out?"

"Sell out?"

"Yes. I've had the pleasure of meeting Favor. She sold your last piece of jewellery around one o'clock, I think she said. I didn't see any jewellery by the time I turned up, apart from what she was still wearing. She had collected some orders as well, if you can believe it. She said you'd come home for a lie down, so I stayed at the fete for a bit. I came across Favor with Emily at the face painting station." Hugo helped her to a chair at the kitchen table. Lorna hadn't said anything. Her fear was subsiding, her heart resuming a regular beat.

"Favor's quite good at that as well, turning all the children into Lion King characters," Hugo said, smiling. "And having the most fun of anyone. Remarkable girl, that Favor."

Thinking about the children and Favor and Emily calmed her, and she cast him a self-conscious smile.

Hugo stroked her hair. "You seem a bit quiet, sweetie. What is it?"

"Just feeling a bit low, I suppose. Nothing serious. Getting ready for the fete and then being in the stall was probably a bit much for my leg."

"Hmm. Well, I'd wanted to take you out to celebrate, and to ask you something, but I guess that's off."

"Ask me something?"

Hugo cradled her hands in his. He leaned over them and kissed them. "Uh-huh." Her hands tingled with the brush of his lips.

"What, then? Go on." She snatched her hands back, making him laugh at her sudden energy.

"Favor would've painted you a tigress, darling girl. But I love how there's no messing about with you. In fact, I love you, full stop."

"Oh, Hugo."

Taking her hands back into his, he said, "I know we haven't spent much time together, but I've been making good use of my time away from you."

"Have you? How?"

"I've made some changes in my business. Hired several fabulous people, completed that massive merger I'd been telling you about. The process actually took about two years, so the timing is serendipitous. Last week, I sold my house."

"My word, you have been a busy boy. A touch secretive, perhaps. But I've been busy, too, you know. Rolling pieces of paper. Sticking a dull antique hatpin into my cast to give myself a scratch. Yelling at my children from the sofa." She felt tearful again, and overwhelmed.

"Lorna, stop. Those are important things, love. The everyday bits that make life good. The kind of life that I want with you."

Lorna's heart began to pound again. "What are you saying, Hugo?"

"That I want you and the children to be mine. I want to marry you."

Lorna looked into his arresting eyes. This was a very special moment, something akin to what she'd always hoped for. Great guy —kind and fun, and good to her kids. So why did she feel so upset?

"I can't."

"Honey, I know this is a surprise. I know we haven't been together long, but I am not one to hesitate. I haven't spent as much time as I'd like with the children, though I was just with them on my own and we got on great." He smiled at her, remembering something. "Don't forget, I am from this village. I've known Simon for years. You're all I've ever wanted in a woman, Lorna, and for some ridiculous reason I am convinced that I can make you happy." He spoke with passion, and her heart began to melt.

She smiled, brushed his hair with her fingers. And then frowned. "I am bad at relationships, Hugo. Men say those kinds of things to me, and then… they go away. I've never figured out why, exactly. Besides, I couldn't imagine living anywhere but here. And I could imagine you living anywhere but here."

Undeterred, Hugo looked at her with wonder, with tenderness in his expression. For a minute, he said nothing. *The man is daft in love with me*, Lorna thought. The thought made her laugh out loud.

"Yes, you should be laughing. Honestly, leaving Burleigh Cross isn't really that difficult," he teased. "I know I've mucked this up.

Although I've been thinking since the start of proposing, my preparations were a bit more on the practical side of things. I should've planned something romantic, and had a boulder of a diamond to shock you with. But when I arrived at the fete and you weren't there, I realised again how much I always want you to be with me, so I couldn't wait any longer, you see?"

"No! Hugo, listen. We really wouldn't work, would we? You think you know me, but you don't. I'd be a huge disappointment. In fact, you really ought to leave. Now. And don't come back." Again she pulled away from him.

"Sorry, love. I am not that easy to strike off. Why couldn't you leave the village?"

"Well. Because. This is our house." She crossed her arms and gazed out the window.

"That's what I was trying to say, before. When you're able to do stairs, we've got to find a place to live that suits us. All of us. My house didn't have enough bedrooms to suit the children, which is why I've sold it. I rather sort of hated living there anyway. It's not a family home, and I am a man who's longed for a family for a long time now."

"You're not listening, Hugo. This has always been our home. You haven't removed yourself from the premises. Why do men not take me seriously when I throw them out?"

"Lorna, as I said, I am a local. One who knows that this is most likely still your mother's house. Sweetie, honestly, she may well come back anytime, with a new Aussie husband in tow! Anyway, Simon's living here and he can look after it. Allow me to be brutal: It's incredibly small, it's in bad nick, and it's not yours. I want to give you your own house."

Lorna felt her face growing hot. Surely it was stress. What was wrong with her? This should seem very romantic. Her frustration threatened to make her cry. She had to get rid of him before she began to blub.

"Okay, Hugo. You're quite right, and thank you for insulting my home. I'll admit, it's not the greatest old place. What you're overlooking is that every time I've jumped into a relationship it comes to tears. Namely, mine." It was the wrong thing to say. Talking about tears, while trying not to cry, proved unhelpful. Her eyes filled.

"Come now," he said with a tender voice, stroking her cheek with light fingers. "I hardly think this is the same situation as you've been in before. Those other blokes, well, for a start, you were far too young when you met Finley's father. And you've already told me that marriage wasn't on the offer with either of them. They weren't serious about giving you a home. You'll see, baby, it'll be different this time. I am committed. Ask your brother. He knows. I'll admit, this is the most impetuous thing I've ever done in my life, because it was basically love at first sight. . . But it'll all come right, if you'll trust yourself to be happy."

"Well, I must admit you're right. This is the first marriage proposal I've had. And if I am honest, I've never liked this rundown old house, but was just so very grateful to have a home without needing to pay rent. But I do have kids to consider, Hugo. Uprooting their lives isn't easy, especially Finley. And I have a job, you know."

"Naturally. We'll look carefully at London schools when we shop for the house, of course. Speaking of, I get along with Finley and Peony a treat, I am sure it's because you've raised them so well. They're lovely. No more single parenting—I'll be a good dad, Lorna. Maybe we'll have a few kids of our own, what do you think?" He moved to the edge of his chair, came closer, and kissed her. "I want to take care of you. Let me. Forget the job and do whatever you like. I know you've loved being home with the children since the accident. So, be a mum, full-time. Be my wife."

She pulled back from him and looked into his eyes again.

"Are you out of excuses yet, love?"

Lorna laughed, as tears spilled down her cheeks. "I believe I am. And by the way, Hugo. I love you, too."

Chapter Twenty-Two

THE EVENING HAD grown chilly as he was working. He put away his tools, and swept the floor. An owl hooted outside, a lonely cry into the new night. He flipped off the lights, and pulled the workshop door closed.

He felt drawn into the darkness of the walled garden. Stalwart blooms had pushed their way among the weeds and brambles, their long stems had arched to catch the autumn's afternoon sun.

Simon walked over to the potting shed, retrieved a light pair of secateurs, and went to a clump of dahlias. They were protected from frost and still thriving. He gathered a bouquet of them, adding fragrant spikes of lavender and snowberry stems. He found a bit of twine in his mum's old potting shed and made a proper bundle. He slipped across the lane to Avalyn's place. He laid the bouquet on her doorstep, and turned to leave.

That's when Gus heard him and began barking from his dog run. The great dog bellowed loudly, and a moment later Simon heard him clear the fence. Gus rounded the edge of the cottage as Avalyn was opening her front door.

"Gus!" she shouted, but the dog was determined to protect his mistress.

"Gus, it's me!" Simon said. Gus recalled Simon's voice and scent and wagged his tail good-naturedly.

"A bit of luck for me," Simon said, ruffling Gus's fur. Avalyn smiled back, but didn't move.

"I am sorry if I disturbed you, Avalyn. On a whim I thought of bringing you some of the late flowers, but it didn't work out for me to leave my romantic offering in secrecy, did it?" Simon laughed, hoping she would say something.

She saw the bouquet lying at her feet. The beauty of the deep red flowers, set against white berries and needles of vivid purple, warmed her heart towards his gesture. "Come in for a cup of tea," she said, throwing open the door.

Simon knew it was best not to let go of Gus's collar, and so made his way into the house holding on to him, the dog wedged between him and Avalyn as he passed through. There wasn't a cheerful fire this evening, but a lamp was burning in Avalyn's bedroom. Taking in the fact that she was wearing a dressing gown, he concluded that she'd been reading in bed.

"Reading anything good?"

She turned on the light above the kitchen table as he sat down. Filling the kettle, she said, "I was looking over my recipe collection."

"Oh." Reflecting on the wonderful meals she'd recently made for his family, meals that were no longer welcome by his sister, he found himself with nothing to say. He also thought again how beautiful she was, no matter that her figure was lost in a thick robe, her hair bound in a loose ponytail and her face free of makeup. He wanted to cross the kitchen and kiss her, but she was talking about her plans, and he was meant to be listening.

"The people at the bakery liked my healthy-recipe muffins at the fete, and they're going to add them to the menu, isn't that fabulous? Only, they want me to help tweak one of the recipes."

"Good on you. If you need someone to test samples, you know where I live." This time, their smiles were easier.

"I've seen your light on late at the workshop. Are you and Finley working on another motorcycle or something?"

"Infinitely better. I am making furniture again."

Her reaction was satisfying. Simon felt pride that she was impressed and glad that she understood the importance of what he'd just said.

"Simon, that's simply wonderful." She handed him a mug of tea and he followed her to the pair of chairs by the fire. He put a hand on her waist, and steered her to the small sofa. She smiled and he felt forgiven. They settled in beside each other.

"How did this come about?"

"The success of the bench for the village green gave me the confidence to try. Then the most extraordinary thing happened. Lorna came into some money."

"Yes, I know about that."

"How?" Simon's heart pounded, hoping for both he and his sister that her answer would cast all suspicion from her relationship with Hugo.

"Hugo knew that I was the first person on the scene. Well, you remember. We weren't able to get in touch with you immediately, so I was at the hospital for a bit with Finley. Hugo wasn't quite sure of the details of the accident, or where it had happened, and by whom Lorna had been treated. So he called me asking for the specifics for their company records, instead of asking Lorna with the potential of encountering some resistance from her. He said something along the lines of it being easier to cash a cheque when you've got it in hand rather than one promised to you from an unproven source."

"I see," Simon said, relief flooding over him. He took a sip of tea. "It's awfully generous of Hugo."

"Well, Lorna has been working very hard, but, as far as I know, this is typical of Hugo's generosity. That's how I met him, you see. I was a dietitian at a hospital in London, and I'd gone back to university to further my study. In the midst of doing research, my colleagues and I came across some wonderful possibilities. Research showed that it was possible to prevent blindness in babies subjected to hunger, with Vitamin A supplements. The goal was to formulate a little vitamin pill that could be ground up and put in the babies' drinks. We had to stop the project as we were out of money. Each student had a few local businesses to canvas, asking for donations for our research from people who'd already donated to the hospital in the past. Hugo had given a large donation for the new children's wing, and so his name was on my list. Naturally, he wanted a quick meeting to see that I wasn't some fly-by-night and to be given a list of my credentials and so on. This vetting was supposed to be done by one of his executives, but the poor man had flu. Instead I met Hugo."

"And he asked you out after business was concluded?" Simon could have dug a hole in the ground and jumped in. He could be treading on very thin ice, given that he'd been ignoring Avalyn of late. And it really was none of his business, especially given that he already knew that Hugo and Avalyn had a very brief dating life together.

But he did want to know.

Avalyn smirked at his abruptness. "Sometimes I can tell that you and Lorna are related."

"Sorry for the question." He looked into his tea, willing the moment to pass. "You needn't answer, of course."

"Not at all." Avalyn told how she unexpectedly met Hugo two weeks later, when he came to the hospital's fundraising dinner. "Both of us are rather punctual, which meant that we arrived at the assigned table before any one else, so of course we sat down together. We started chatting and he told me about someone he knew who was acting in a play. It sounded interesting, and I said so, and he asked me to join him. We didn't really interact much at the play, so we gave it another go some weeks later, when we went to dinner and then a concert. Dinner was miserable. The concert was loud, alternative stuff, and my taste runs to instrumental and pop, you see, and that's when it was confirmed that we really are better as friends-who-raise-funds."

"I was sort of puzzled by something."

"What's that?" Avalyn leaned towards him, obviously longing to be open, wanting to help them get beyond this rough patch. But what Simon wanted to ask sounded nothing but accusatory.

"Well, it's just that you'd heard Lorna mention Miss Harrop. It seemed a bit odd you didn't mention having gone out with Hugo."

Avalyn looked shocked and laughed. He thought again, how

lovely she was, and felt spellbound by her merry laughter.

"Simon Whiston. You've been jealous!"

He thought for a moment about this. "Yes, I suppose I have."

"Darling man," she said, tracing her finger along his cheekbone and jaw. "I didn't keep Hugo a secret. Consider this from my point of view, will you? I knew him terribly briefly, about four years ago. I never really got to know him. Not only did I fail to make the name connection until sometime after hearing it several times, but you'd said you'd grown up with Hugo in the village. And I only realised sometime later that Lorna somehow managed to never meet him properly, I gathered that was because of their age difference. So, I ask you—what was I meant to add to the conversation? You had known him for years, and Lorna was dating him. It seemed irrelevant that I'd seen him three or four times in the whole of my life, and he really wasn't mentioned during those family times, when we were gathered at the table."

"Hmm, alright. But—"

"Simon!"

"Sorry. When did he bring you to Burleigh Cross?"

She let an exasperated sigh escape, and told him. "Ironically, the play we saw was at that small community theatre in Stonewyck, so we drove through Burleigh Cross, and I always remembered the *Twinns* at the village entrance, so it was easy to find the village again."

"Oh, right. The actor Hugo mentioned. He would've been a chap we went to school with, called Colin Jones."

"I don't remember the actor's name, but most likely you're right. You've been building a kingdom in your mind with regards to of all this–you and your sister–haven't you? Is that why she's so cross with me?"

He grinned. "We are quite irritating. I see that rather clearly, now."

"And gorgeous, too."

He took her tea and his, and stood the mugs on the small table in front of them. Avalyn met him halfway for a kiss.

Chapter Twenty-Three

SPRING

FINLEY SAT at the kitchen table, his head nestled deeply into his forearms. His Uncle Simon was making sandwiches for their Saturday afternoon lunch. His sister, Peony, played on the floor, singing a little song to her fairy doll as she wrapped her up in a piece of paper. She had decorated the paper dress using every crayon in the box.

Outside, the spring sunshine glazed the windows with a cheerful glow, and Finley could hear the birds singing over the voicemails that were coming out of Uncle Simon's phone. The phone was on speaker, resting on a tea towel and squawking away, as his uncle replaced the top piece of bread on his new creations. Instead of crisps, Finley knew Uncle Simon would put baby carrots and dill dip on their plates because Avalyn liked them to eat vegetables and things. Finley didn't care what they were served for lunch. He just wanted his life to stay the same. He wanted to stay here, in Burleigh Cross.

Uncle Simon was tying off the bread and putting things back in the fridge when the next message played.

"Simon, this is Guy Trench. I suppose you'll remember speaking with me at the autumn fete this past year. About the Panther? I've got the money now, you see, and if you've still got the bike for sale, I'd be interested. Give me a ring back either way, alright? Cheers."

Finley's eyes squeezed back tears inside the sweaty, safe darkness he'd created on the kitchen table's surface, with his face surrounded by his arms. He inhaled the oaky smell of the table, the wood surface inches from his nose and mouth. Mum and Hugo would probably have some new posh kind of table in their new house in London. Not a good smelling, old table like this, where three generations of his family had eaten their meals. He knew that things weren't always rosy for his mum and Uncle Simon growing up, and that Grandpa was a drinker. But, still, this had been home to them all. And it was the only home he'd ever known. Leaving the farmhouse, and selling off the motorcycle, clearly signified that life as he knew it was drawing to a close.

He sensed a change in the air on the back of his neck as his Uncle Simon stepped close, and then the strange cavernous echo across the table's surface as his uncle set down three luncheon plates and glasses of milk. He told Peony to lay her doll aside. Finley would have to raise his head to the blinding light, and keep living. He wasn't sure he could.

Peony was mooing Gemma and running towards the table. As she jumped into her chair, she made the table jolt slightly beneath Fin's face. That angered him beyond reason, and he snapped up his head and glared at his sister.

"Hey, why so glum mate?"

Fin wiped sweat, and maybe a tear, from his cheek, and ignored his uncle.

"Fin?"

"Nothing."

They said grace and began eating. At least, his sister and his uncle began eating. Finley was hungry, and his sandwich was appealing. But since he was doomed to leaving his mates, quitting his home, and moving to some smelly city, he thought starvation might be a noble solution. There weren't carrots on his plate as expected. Instead, spring peas that had been lightly microwaved. They'd be tender, slightly crunchy and unbelievably sweet. He longed to put a pat of butter on the steaming peas and eat them all up.

"Mmm. Avalyn's peas are awfully good," said Uncle Simon.

Curse your eyes, thought Finley. He was fairly certain that rebelling through starvation would be easier once the peas were taken away. Peony had put down her spoon, even though if Mum were here she wouldn't have let her, and was eating the peas one by precious one, and giggling at him all the while. He wouldn't miss his little sister when he was dead.

"Something you want to talk about, Fin?"

Finley shot his uncle the meanest look he could muster. It was a little frightening. He hadn't ever been seriously cheeky to his uncle before, and he wasn't sure that he wouldn't get a backhand across the face or something. That seemed far scarier than his impending death, which he'd learned at school could be accomplished fairly quickly, perhaps inside a week, particularly if he didn't take any water. Water always factored in hugely when you were dying.

"You'll refrain from giving me looks like that, if you know what's good for you."

Finley immediately diverted his eyes. Horribly, the tears were coming back, and they were no longer for a motorcycle, but coming from a really deep place in his chest. In other words, he knew he was about to cry like a little girl. Life could not get any worse.

He meant to say something, but when he tried, water started coming out of his eyes, and his face twisted up and a big sort of honking noise come out of his nose, blowing snot and sending Peony into a shriek of laughter.

Then his uncle did something remarkably weird. Uncle Simon put down his sandwich, backed his chair away from the table, knelt by his chair and pulled Finley by the shoulders. Finley ended up in a face plant against his uncle's neck, where he sobbed like a baby. When he'd done, his uncle was stroking his hair, just like his Mum always had done, and then he handed Finley a tea towel to blow his nose and wipe his face upon, which his Mum never would have done. Finley did this, and slumped back into his chair.

Then Finley began to eat his peas, which popped gloriously in his mouth.

***

The day droned on, and Finley had a headache from his baby-crying episode at lunch. He was in bed for the night, looking up at the spring moon through his bedroom window. His room was small, but it was plenty big enough for his bed and a little desk, and had loads of football posters on every wall, even a small one above the door with half of it creased to follow right up the lean in the ceiling. He heard his uncle's tread coming up the stairs, and wondered what he was doing. Uncle Simon still slept in the box room, even though Mum was away. A moment later, there was a soft knock on Fin's door, and his uncle came and sat on the bed.

The bed was narrow and Finley backed closer to the wall, to give Uncle Simon enough room to perch. Finley marvelled at how heavy the man was, the mattress heaving toward the floor with his weight. He wondered if he would be as tall as his uncle when he grew up. He realised that he'd never known what his own father was like–short or tall, fair or dark, or anything else– but it never seemed to matter much because he looked like Mum and her brother, and like pictures of his grandfather.

"Want to talk about it, Fin?"

Finley did want to talk about it. But he didn't know how to begin. He was glad, though, that his uncle hadn't turned on the light. The moonlight was bright, but if he cried again it wouldn't be quite as humiliating.

"Well, there's something I've wanted to say to you, all day."

Finley wasn't afraid to hear what his uncle wanted to say. His voice was kind and he wasn't speaking overly loud or acting as though he were being cheerful, like some adults do trying to make you feel as though everything horrible is a fun game of some sort.

"I called that bloke back, the one who wanted to buy the Panther. Do you know what I told him?"

"No." Fin squeaked his reply.

"I told him that my nephew's motorcycle wasn't for sale. I told him, whether he cared to hear it or not, that I was counting on my nephew to come visit me from London, and that it would be here for him when he did."

"You did?"

"Of course, Fin. And you will come back to Burleigh Cross and ride it, and send fear and trembling to anyone walking about the green when you go thundering past."

His uncle smiled and tousled Fin's hair. "That's one thing settled, then."

"Yes."

"And I expect now that the time's getting close, you're not quite sure if you want to go through with moving away?"

Finley's heart lifted with hope. Perhaps he had a choice, and moving to London was something he didn't have to do? Was his uncle going to ask him to go on living with him, here at the farmhouse?

"I don't want to go through with it," Finley replied. "I want to live here. Forever."

Uncle Simon laid his hand on Finley's shoulder, and again Finley's eyes pricked with tears. It was a gesture of solace, and Finley knew that his uncle wasn't going to invite him to stay.

"Don't you like Hugo?"

Finley sniffed, and ran his pajama sleeve across his eyes. "He's alright. Mum's crazy about him. I am chuffed for her. But I don't see why we can't stay here. Hugo's from here, and they could live here after they get married. It's not a bad place. They're not thinking of anyone else but themselves. They don't care if Peony and me don't like it."

"I suppose your mum figured you were more like me."

"What do y'mean?" Finley had expected to have a debate about how much Mum loved him and things like that.

"I couldn't wait to leave the village and go to London. Same as Hugo. You're getting to go before your twelfth birthday. Rather lucky, wouldn't you say?"

"No. Because you wanted to come back to Burleigh Cross. And you didn't have to go to school in the city. You'd already finished, before you got to London."

"Oh, is that how you figure it? The truth is, Fin, I never wanted to come back to Burleigh Cross. But I'd lost my home and my business, and had nowhere else to go. I am glad of it, now, as I love all of you, and I wanted us to be family. But I promise you, you'll make new friends and the new school will be much easier when that happens. London's a cool place. And you'll finally have a father. Hugo is keen to make you happy, you know. And your mum's getting a smart new house—well as of yesterday, in fact. She called and said they signed off the paperwork and were given the key. She's getting the house ready for you and Peony, and packing new clothes for you, for your trip. You're even getting a huge, new, double bed, instead of having to put this one on a lorry and move it to London."

"I like *this* bed. And what if you're wrong? What if I hate it?"

"I was just coming to that."

"You were?" Finley didn't know what his uncle was going to say, but he'd already felt a bit better. Hugo had shown him where boys his age played footie, and it was only two streets away from the new house he was buying for them. And the school was closer than going to the village, on the other side of a park that sort of made it seem like crossing the village green, only a lot bigger.

"Fin, one of the best things I've learned is to live one day at a time. Do you know what I mean?"

"Not exactly."

"Tomorrow when you're back from school, and Peony goes to Emily's house, you and I can ride the motorcycle. Are you looking forward to it?"

"Sure."

"The idea is for you to aim at having all the fun that's humanly possible tomorrow. And this week, before the term ends, you should have all of the fun you still can, with your mates. You're not to think of anything else but what you're doing today, and everything that is good or brings the most fun."

"You're saying that I'll miss all the fun, if I am worrying about my new school now."

"I always said you were an intelligent boy. Like your uncle. And then when you leave your school, you'll enjoy your adventure of going to Australia, and visiting Granny, and going to Mum and Hugo's wedding there, too."

"I've wanted to go to Australia since Granny left."

"You'll have the time of your life down there."

"And you'll get on okay? Who'll help you with the furniture?"

"Don't worry about me, Fin. I feel strong, and now that I am selling furniture at a good clip again, I can afford to hire help if I have some bad days. But like you, I am going to be enjoying one day at a time, especially having that pretty woman just across the road."

Finley felt better than he imagined he could, since starving himself at the beginning of lunch. Not only had they had pizza for supper, his favourite, but now he was a bit more excited about his new life. He thought Uncle Simon seemed excited, too. He wondered what his Granny would cook them for Easter lunch, and how many kangaroos they would see. They talked for a while longer. Uncle Simon said goodnight, and as he left Finley's room, Finley turned over in his soft bed and settled in for a good sleep.

Chapter Twenty-Four

AVALYN STOOD BEHIND Simon, her arms circling his waist, and watched with him through the window as Hugo's new Mercedes pulled out into the lane. "I am a family man, now," Hugo had said with obvious delight, showing the MPV to Simon earlier this morning. "Needed a larger vehicle for the precious cargo."

"It's a wonder you've any more room for the children, what with all those cases," Simon had said, closing the passenger's door after his inspection. "Lorna's obviously packed for a three week's stay that wouldn't include laundering any clothes."

Hugo laughed. Simon's sister could obviously do no wrong in her fiancé's opinion. "We've got a lot of extra clobber for our wedding, though, so we may be a bit lighter coming back. Or not. Depends if I take her shopping, I suppose."

"And how much food our mother tries to send with you on the return flight."

Their farewell hadn't seemed like a goodbye as much as a bon voyage, as Hugo, Lorna, Finley, and Peony were excited about their wedding and holiday at Granny's in Melbourne. Finley had shown none of the reservations he'd suffered with over the past week, and Peony was elated to see her Mummy. Simon was pleasantly surprised to hear Peony call Hugo, "Daddy." Hugo was so pleased that he kissed her cheek, nose, or forehead every time the little girl addressed him as such. Lorna had found time for a quick word with her brother in the kitchen, whilst Hugo and the children told Avalyn how many hours they would fly, and how they would rent a car when they landed, and what time they figured it might be, and whether or not Granny would be able to sleep tonight, knowing that they were on their way.

"Thank you for taking care of the children this past week, Simon. It meant the world for Finley to be able to finish out the term, and for Hugo and I to get everything done before leaving."

"My pleasure, Sis. I miss you all, already."

"Me, too," Lorna said, hugging him. "You'll be alright, won't you?"

"Of course. I've got plenty of work to keep me busy, and Avalyn to keep me company."

"You won't overdo?"

"No, love. I am never going to sacrifice my health or happiness again. My next furniture empire will have me doing things a bit differently. For the moment, Vandersteen's delighted and he's paid me another lovely, fat sum, but I'll take on help, soon, and work reasonable hours."

"I am glad to hear it, Simon. I can't wait for you to see our new house. The pictures I sent don't do it justice. You'll come and visit when we get back?"

"Well, perhaps when you've had a couple of weeks to settle in," Simon promised.

"And you can bring Avalyn."

"Oh, I'll have to," he said with a smile. "She'll need to show me what sort of ring she'd like."

Lorna's face lit up like a Christmas tree. He hoped Avalyn would be at least half as excited as his sister. "Simon! Does she know, yet?"

"No. And I want to surprise her. Thought I'd take her to my favourite old haunts in London, make a day of it. A fancy dinner and ask her afterwards, while strolling in the park. Or something along those lines. Then we'll probably buy the ring at a little shop I know of on Brompton Road."

"I couldn't be more thrilled for you, both!" Lorna said. Simon could see she was imagining joyful things, perhaps family gatherings in the future, and her eyes misted with happiness.

"You were right about her, you know. She is capable of working magic." They laughed together, and Lorna hugged him, again, and he returned her embrace, free of the pain of the past.

When the four of them left, Simon thought they already looked like a natural family. Hugo had put Peony in her car seat and then waited patiently while Lorna had given another round of hugs to he and Avalyn. Finley was obviously pleased, the excitement of taking his first plane ride gave him a broad grin. Seeing them together made Simon determined he'd never loose touch with his family again.

Now he turned to the beautiful woman standing next to him, and found that she was crying. "You and my sister are speeding towards dehydration," he teased.

Avalyn ran her fingers through his hair. "You haven't told me, yet."

"Told you what?"

"You said that, come spring, you'd share your fantastic plans for refurbishing your Mum's garden."

"Yes, I did. Let's walk out there and I'll give you a tour from my imagination."

Avalyn laughed, and they walked towards the garden, to talk about the future.

For more information, and to sign-up for announcements about upcoming books, please visit www.MicheleDeppe.com

Made in the USA
Lexington, KY
18 December 2014